International praise for

VINEGAR GIRL

"A screwball comedy of manners that actually channels Jane Austen more than Shakespeare. It's clear that [Tyler] had fun with *Vinegar Girl,* and readers will too. . . . A fizzy cocktail of a romantic comedy, far more sweet than acidic, about finding a mate who appreciates you for your idiosyncratic, principled self—no taming necessary."

—NPR.org

"An effective retelling, while nodding to the original text, stands on its own as a story in the way Iris Murdoch's *The Black Prince* responds to *Hamlet* and Aldous Huxley's *Brave New World* plays with *The Tempest.* Tyler succeeds in creating a world we believe in. . . . Charming . . . clever."

—*Boston Globe*

"A perfect read."

—*New York Post*

"*Vinegar Girl* is a fast, easy read. . . . Held side-by-side against Shakespeare's *Shrew,* the story of Kate and Pyotr is full of hidden treasures."

—*Houston Chronicle*

"*Vinegar Girl* has the requisite Tyler trademarks. . . . The characters populating *Vinegar Girl* are flawed, quirky, likable, self-indulgent and astute."

—*St. Louis Post-Dispatch*

"Family drama meets rom-com in a modern version of *The Taming of the Shrew*. Pushy dad plus entitled little sister, cute but clueless suitor, and Pulitzer Prize–winning author equals must-read."

—*Cosmopolitan*

"Is there any living American writer who has written as well about marriage as Anne Tyler? Or who has consistently been as honest about the disconnect between fantasies of lovebirds living happily ever after and the often sad but also funny miracle of two separate people actually staying together? In *Vinegar Girl* Tyler brings these talents to the altar of the Hogarth Shakespeare series . . . it's fun, lighthearted, clever, compassionate and filled with Tyler's always extraordinary love for her characters, liberating them here to love each other."

—*Milwaukee Journal-Sentinel*

"A great success; *Vinegar Girl* is funny and endearing, the quirky characters vintage Tyler."

—*Minneapolis Star Tribune*

"A very funny retelling of Shakespeare's *The Taming of the Shrew*."

—*Sacramento Bee*

consistently finds good in unpromising people and is a sharp and very funny observer of day-to-day life. . . . A joy."

—*Literary Review*

"Excellent."

—*Glamour*

"A reflective, engaging twist on Shakespeare's unfashionable play."

—*Daily Express*

THE
HOGARTH
SHAKESPEARE

VINEGAR GIRL

VINEGAR GIRL

William Shakespeare's
The Taming of the Shrew Retold

ANNE TYLER

THE HOGARTH SHAKESPEARE

VINTAGE CANADA

VINTAGE CANADA EDITION, 2017

Copyright © 2016 by Anne Tyler
Readers Group Guide copyright © 2017 by
Penguin Random House LLC

Published by Vintage Canada, a division of Penguin Random House Canada Limited, in 2017. Originally published in hardcover by Knopf Canada, a division of Penguin Random House Canada Limited, in 2016, and simultaneously in the United States by Hogarth, an imprint of the Crown Publishing Group, a division of Penguin Random House LLC, New York, and in Great Britain by Hogarth UK, a division of the Random House Group Limited, a Penguin Random House Company, London. Distributed in Canada by Penguin Random House Canada Limited, Toronto.

Vintage Canada with colophon is a registered trademark.

www.penguinrandomhouse.ca

Library and Archives Canada Cataloguing in Publication

Tyler, Anne, author
    Vinegar girl : the taming of the shrew retold / Anne Tyler.

(Hogarth Shakespeare)

ISBN 978-0-345-80915-5   eBook ISBN 978-0-345-80916-2

    I. Shakespeare, William, 1564–1616. Taming of the shrew. I. Title.

PS3570.Y45V56 2017   813'.54   C2015-908541-1

Text design by Lauren Dong
Cover images: (man) Erin Patrice O'Brien, (grass) Corbis/VCG, (petals) Fabian Krause/EyeEm, all Getty Images; (woman) Vanessa Chambard/plainpicture

Printed and bound in the United States of America

2 4 6 8 9 7 5 3 1

 Penguin
Random
House

VINEGAR GIRL

CHAPTER ONE

KATE BATTISTA WAS GARDENING OUT BACK WHEN she heard the telephone ring in the kitchen. She straightened up and listened. Her sister was in the house, although she might not be awake yet. But then there was another ring, and two more after that, and when she finally heard her sister's voice it was only the announcement on the answering machine. "Hi-yee! It's us? We're not home, looks like? So leave a—"

By that time Kate was striding toward the back steps, tossing her hair off her shoulders with an exasperated "Tcch!" She wiped her hands on her jeans and yanked the screen door open. "Kate," her father was saying, "pick up."

She lifted the receiver. "What," she said.

"I forgot my lunch."

Her eyes went to the counter beside the fridge where, sure enough, his lunch sat precisely where she had set it the night before. She always used those clear plastic bags that supermarket produce came in, and the contents were plainly visible: a Tupperware sandwich box and an apple. "Huh," she said.

"Can you bring it?"

"Bring it *now*?"

"Right."

"Jesus, Father. I'm not the Pony Express," she said.

"What else have you got to do?" he asked her.

"It's Sunday! I'm weeding the hellebores."

"Ah, Kate, don't be like that. Just hop in the car and zip over; there's a good girl."

"Sheesh," she said, and she slammed the receiver down and took the lunch bag from the counter.

There were several strange things about this conversation. The first was that it had happened at all; her father distrusted the telephone. In fact, his lab didn't even *have* a telephone, so he must have called on his cell phone. And that was unusual too, because his only reason for owning a cell phone was that his daughters had insisted. He had gone into a brief flurry of app purchases when he first acquired it—scientific calculators of various types, for the most part—and after that had lost all interest, and avoided it now altogether.

Then there was the fact that he forgot his lunch about twice a week, but had never before seemed to notice. The man did not eat, basically. Kate would get home from work and find his lunch still sitting on the counter, and yet even so she would have to shout for him three or four times that evening before he would come to dinner. Always he had something better to do, some journal to read or notes to go over. He would probably starve to death if he were living alone.

And supposing he did feel a bit peckish, he could have just stepped out and bought something. His lab was near the Johns Hopkins campus, and there were sandwich shops and convenience stores everywhere you looked.

Not to mention that it wasn't even noon yet.

But the day was sunny and breezy, if cool—the first semi-decent weather after a long, hard, bitter winter—and she didn't actually mind an excuse to get out in the world. She wouldn't take the car, though; she would walk. Let him wait. (He himself *never* took the car, unless he had some sort of equipment to ferry. He was something of a health fiend.)

She stepped out the front door, shutting it extra hard behind her because it irked her that Bunny was sleeping so late. The ground cover along the front walk had a twiggy, littered look, and she made a mental note to spruce it up after she finished with the hellebores.

Swinging the lunch bag by its twist-tied neck, she passed the Mintzes' house and the Gordons' house—stately brick center-hall Colonials like the Battistas' own, although better maintained—and turned the corner. Mrs. Gordon was kneeling among her azalea bushes, spreading mulch around their roots. "Why, hello there, Kate!" she sang out.

"Hi."

"Looks like spring might be thinking of coming!"

"Yup."

Kate strode on without slowing, her buckskin jacket flying out behind her. A pair of young women—most likely Hopkins students—drifted at a snail's pace ahead of her. "I could tell he wanted to ask me," one was saying, "because he kept clearing his throat in that way they do, you know? But then not speaking."

"I love when they're so shy," the other one said.

Kate veered around them and kept going.

At the next street she took a left, heading toward a more mixed-and-mingled neighborhood of apartments and small cafés and houses partitioned into offices, and eventually she turned in at yet another brick Colonial. This one had a smaller front yard than the Battistas' but a larger, grander portico. Six or eight plaques beside the front door spelled out the names of various offbeat organizations and obscure little magazines. There was no plaque for Louis Battista, though. He had been shunted around to so many different buildings over the years, landing finally in this orphan location near the university but miles from the medical complex, that he'd probably decided it just wasn't worth the effort.

In the foyer an array of mailboxes lined one wall, and sliding heaps of flyers and takeout menus covered the rickety bench beneath them. Kate walked past several offices, but only the Christians for Buddha door stood open. Inside she glimpsed a trio of women grouped around a desk where a fourth woman sat dabbing her eyes with a tissue. (Always *something* going on.) Kate opened another door at the far end of the hall and descended a flight of steep wooden stairs. At the bottom she paused to punch in the code: 1957, the date Witebsky first defined the criteria for autoimmune disorders.

The room she entered was tiny, furnished only by a card table and two metal folding chairs. A brown paper bag sat on the table; another lunch, it looked like. She set her father's lunch next to it and then went over to a door and gave a couple of brisk knocks. After a moment, her father poked his head out—his satiny bald scalp bordered by a narrow band of black hair, his olive-skinned face punctuated by a black mustache and round-lensed, rimless spectacles. "Ah, Kate," he said. "Come in."

"No, thanks," she said. She never could abide the smells of the place—the thin, stinging smell of the lab itself and the dry-paper smell of the mouse room. "Your lunch is on the table," she said. "Bye."

"No, wait!"

He turned from her to speak to someone in the room behind him. "Pyoder? Come out and say hello to my daughter."

"I've got to go," Kate said.

"I don't think you've ever met my research assistant," her father said.

"That's okay."

But the door opened wider, and a solid, muscular man with straight yellow hair stepped up to stand next to her father. His white lab coat was so dingy that it very nearly matched Dr. Battista's pale-gray coveralls. "Vwouwv!" he said. Or that was what it sounded like, at least. He was gazing at Kate admiringly. Men often wore that look when they first saw her. It was due to a bunch of dead cells: her hair, which was blue-black and billowy and extended below her waist.

"This is Pyoder Cherbakov," her father told her.

"Pyotr," the man corrected him, allowing no space at all between the sharp-pointed *t* and the ruffly, rolling *r*. And "Shcherbakov," explosively spitting out the mishmash of consonants.

"Pyoder, meet Kate."

"Hi," Kate said. "See you later," she told her father.

"I thought you might stay a moment."

"What for?"

"Well, you'll need to take back my sandwich box, will you not?"

"Well, you can bring it back yourself, can you not?"

A sudden hooting sound made both of them glance in Pyotr's direction. "Just like the girls in my country," he said, beaming. "So rude-spoken."

"Just like the *women*," Kate said reprovingly.

"Yes, they also. The grandmothers and the aunties."

She gave up on him. "Father," she said, "will you tell Bunny she has to stop leaving such a mess when she has her friends in? Did you see the TV room this morning?"

"Yes, yes," her father said, but he was heading back into the lab as he spoke. He returned, pushing a high stool on wheels. He parked it next to the table. "Have a seat," he told her.

"I need to get back to my gardening."

"Please, Kate," he said. "You never keep me company."

She stared at him. "Keep you *company*?"

"Sit, sit," he said, motioning toward the stool. "You can have part of my sandwich."

"I'm not hungry," she said. But she perched awkwardly on the stool, still staring at him.

"Pyoder, sit. You can share my sandwich too, if you want. Kate made it especially. Peanut butter honey on whole-wheat."

"You know I do not eat peanut butter," Pyotr told

him severely. He pulled out one of the folding chairs and settled catty-corner to Kate. His chair was considerably lower than her stool, and she could see how the hair was starting to thin across the top of his head. "In my country, peanuts are pigs' food."

"Ha, ha," Dr. Battista said. "He's very humorous, isn't he, Kate?"

"What?"

"They eat them with the shells on," Pyotr said.

He had trouble with *th* sounds, Kate noticed. And his vowels didn't seem to last long enough. She had no patience with foreign accents.

"Were you surprised that I used my cell phone?" her father asked her. He was still standing, for some reason. He pulled his phone from a pocket in his coveralls. "You girls were right; it comes in handy," he said. "I'm going to start using it more often now." He frowned down at it for a moment, as if he were trying to remember what it was. Then he punched a button and held it in front of his face. Squinting, he took several steps backward. There was a mechanical clicking sound. "See? It takes photographs," he said.

"Erase it," Kate ordered.

"I don't know how," he said, and the phone clicked again.

"Damn it, Father, sit down and eat. I need to get back to my gardening."

"All right, all right."

He tucked the phone away and sat down. Pyotr, meanwhile, was opening his lunch bag. He pulled out two eggs and then a banana and placed them on the flattened paper bag in front of him. "Pyoder believes in bananas," Dr. Battista confided. "I keep telling him about apples, but does he listen?" He was opening his own lunch bag, taking out his apple. "Pectin! Pectin!" he told Pyotr, shaking the apple under Pyotr's nose.

"Bananas are miracle food," Pyotr said calmly, and he picked his up and started peeling it. He had a face that was almost hexagonal, Kate noticed—his cheekbones widening to two sharp points, the angles of his jaw two more points slanting to the point of his chin, and the long strands of his hair separating over his forehead to form the topmost point. "Also eggs," he was saying. "The egg of the hen! So cleverly self-contained."

"Kate makes my sandwich for me every single night before she goes to bed," Dr. Battista said. "She's very domestic."

Kate blinked.

"Peanut butter, though," Pyotr said.

"Well, yes."

"Yes," Pyotr said with a sigh. He sent her a look of regret. "But is certainly *pretty* enough."

"You should see her sister."

Kate said, "Oh! Father!"

"What?"

"This sister is where?" Pyotr asked.

"Well, Bunny is only fifteen. She's still in high school."

"Okay," Pyotr said. He returned his gaze to Kate.

Kate wheeled her stool back sharply and stood up. "Don't forget your Tupperware," she told her father.

"What! You're leaving? Why so soon?"

But Kate just said, "Bye"—mostly addressing Pyotr, who was watching her with a measuring look—and she marched to the door and flung it open.

"Katherine, dearest, don't rush off!" Her father stood up. "Oh, dear, this isn't going well at all. It's just that she's so busy, Pyoder. I can never get her to sit down and take a little break. Did I tell you she runs our whole house? She's very domestic. Oh, I already said that. And she has a full-time job besides. Did I tell you she teaches preschool? She's wonderful with small children."

"Why are you *talking* this way?" Kate demanded, turning on him. "What's come over you? I hate small children; you know that."

There was another hooting sound from Pyotr. He was grinning up at her. "Why you hate small children?" he asked her.

"Well, they're not very bright, if you've noticed."

He hooted again. What with his hooting and the banana he held, he reminded her of a chimpanzee. She spun away and stalked out, letting the door slam shut, and climbed the stairs two at a time.

Behind her, she heard the door open again. Her father called, "Kate?" She heard his steps on the stairs, but she strode on toward the front of the building.

His steps softened as he arrived on the carpet. "I'll just see you out, why don't I?" he called after her.

See her out?

But she paused when she reached the front door. She turned to watch him approach.

"I've handled things badly," he said. He smoothed his scalp with one palm. His coveralls were one-size-fits-all and they ballooned in the middle, giving him the look of a Teletubby. "I didn't mean to make you angry," he said.

"I'm not angry; I'm . . ."

But she couldn't say the word "hurt." It might bring tears to her eyes. "I'm fed up," she said instead.

"I don't understand."

She could believe that, actually. Face it: he was clueless.

"And what were you trying to do back there?" she asked him, setting her fists on her hips. "Why were you acting so . . . peculiar with that assistant?"

"He's not 'that assistant'; he's Pyoder Cherbakov, whom I'm very lucky to have. Just look: he came in on a Sunday! He does that often. And he's been with me nearly three years, by the way, so I would think you would at least be familiar with his name."

"Three years? What happened to Ennis?"

"Good Lord! Ennis! Ennis was two assistants back."

"Oh," she said.

She didn't know why he was acting so irritable. It wasn't as if he ever talked about his assistants—or about anything, in fact.

"I seem to have a little trouble keeping them," he said. "It may be that to outsiders, my project is not looking very promising."

This wasn't something he had admitted before, although from time to time Kate had wondered. It made her feel sorry for him, suddenly. She let her hands drop to her sides.

"I went to a great deal of effort to bring Pyoder to this country," he said. "I don't know if you realize. He was only twenty-five at the time, but everybody who's anybody in autoimmunity had heard of him. He's brilliant. He qualified for an O-1 visa, and that's not something you often see these days."

"Well, good, Father."

"An extraordinary-ability visa; that's what an O-1 is. It means that he possesses some extraordinary skill or knowledge that no one here in this country has, and that I am involved in some extraordinary research that justifies my needing him."

"Good for you."

"O-1 visas last three years."

She reached out to touch his forearm. "Of *course* you're anxious about your project," she said, in what she hoped was an encouraging tone. "But I bet things will be fine."

"You really think so?" he asked.

She nodded and gave his arm a couple of clumsy pats, which he must not have been expecting because he looked startled. "I'm sure of it," she told him. "Don't forget to bring your sandwich box home."

Then she opened the front door and walked out into the sunshine. Two of the Christians for Buddha women were sitting on the steps with their heads together. They were laughing so hard about something that it took them a moment to notice her, but then they drew apart to let her pass.

CHAPTER TWO

THE LITTLE GIRLS IN ROOM 4 WERE PLAYING breakup. The ballerina doll was breaking up with the sailor doll. "I'm sorry, John," she said in a brisk, business-like voice—Jilly's voice, actually—"but I'm in love with somebody else."

"Who?" the sailor doll asked. It was Emma G. who was speaking for him, holding him up by the waist of his little blue middy blouse.

"I can't tell you who, on account of he's your best friend and so it would hurt your feelings."

"Well, that's just stupid," Emma B. pointed out from the sidelines. "Now he knows anyhow, since you said it was his best friend."

"He could have a whole bunch of best friends, though."

"No, he couldn't. Not if they were 'best.'"

"Yes, he could. Me, I have four best friends."

"You're a weirdo, then."

"Kate! Did you hear what she called me?"

"What do you care?" Kate asked. She was helping Ja-meesha take her painting smock off. "Tell her she's weird herself."

"You're weird yourself," Jilly told Emma B.

"Am not."

"Are so."

"Am not."

"Kate said you were, so there!"

"I didn't say that," Kate said.

"Did so."

Kate was about to say, "Did not," but she changed it to, "Well, anyhow, I wasn't the one who started it."

They were gathered in the doll corner—seven little girls and the Samson twins, Raymond and David. In another corner all six of the remaining boys were crowded at the sand table, which they had contrived to turn into a sports arena. They were using a plastic spoon to catapult Lego bricks into a fluted metal Jell-O mold that had been positioned at the far end. Most of the time they missed, but whenever anyone scored a hit there would be a burst of cheers, and then the others would start elbowing one another aside and wrestling for control of the spoon so that they could try for themselves.

Kate should go over and quiet them down, but she didn't. Let them work off some of that energy, she figured. Besides, she was not, in fact, the teacher; she was the teacher's assistant—a world of difference.

The Charles Village Little People's School had been founded forty-five years ago by Mrs. Edna Darling, who still ran it, and all of her teachers were old enough that they required assistants—one assistant apiece, and two for the more labor-intensive two-year-old class—because who could expect them to chase around after a gang of little rapscallions at their advanced stage of life? The school occupied the basement level of Aloysius Church, but it was aboveground, mostly, so the rooms were sunlit and cheerful, with a set of double doors opening directly onto the playground. The end farthest from the doors had been walled off to form a faculty lounge where the older women spent large blocks of time drinking herbal tea and discussing their physical declines. Sometimes the assistants would venture into the lounge for a cup of tea themselves, or to use the faculty restroom with its grown-up-size sink and toilet; but always they had the sense that they were interrupting a private meeting, and they tended not to linger even though the teachers were cordial to them.

To put it mildly, it had never been Kate's plan to work in a preschool. However, during her sophomore year in college she had told her botany professor that his explanation of photosynthesis was "half-assed." One thing had led to another, and eventually she was invited to leave. She had worried about her father's reaction, but after he'd heard the whole story he said, "Well, you were right: it *was* half-assed," and that was the end of it. So there she was, back home with nothing to do until her aunt Thelma stepped in and arranged for a position at the school. (Aunt Thelma was on the board there. She was on many boards.) In theory Kate could have applied for readmission to her college the following year, but she somehow didn't. It had probably slipped her father's mind that she had the option, even, and certainly it was easier for him to have her around to run things and look after her little sister, who was only five at the time but already straining the abilities of their ancient housekeeper.

The teacher Kate assisted was named Mrs. Chauncey. (All the teachers were "Mrs." to their assistants.) She was a comfortable, extremely overweight woman who had been tending four-year-olds longer than Kate had been alive. Ordinarily she treated them with a benign absent-mindedness, but when one of them misbehaved, it was "Connor Fitzgerald, I *see* what you're up to!" and "Emma Gray, Emma Wills: eyes front!" She thought that Kate was too lax with them. If a child refused to lie down at Quiet Rest Time, Kate just said, "Fine, be that way," and stomped off in a huff. Mrs. Chauncey would send her a reproachful look before telling the child, "*Somebody* isn't doing what Miss Kate told him to." At such moments, Kate felt like an impostor. Who was she to order a child to take a nap? She completely lacked authority, and all the children knew it; they seemed to view her as just an extra-tall, more obstreperous four-year-old. Not once during her six years at the school had the students themselves addressed her as "Miss Kate."

From time to time Kate entertained the notion of looking for work elsewhere, but it never came to anything. She didn't interview well, to be honest. And anyhow, she couldn't think what she might be qualified to do instead.

In her coed dorm back in college she had once been drawn into a game of chess in the common room. Kate was not very good at chess, but she was an audacious player, reckless and unorthodox, and she managed to keep her opponent on the defensive for some time. A small crowd of her dorm mates gathered around the board to watch, but Kate paid them no attention until she overheard what the boy behind her whispered to someone standing next to him. "She has. No. Plan," he whispered. Which was true, in fact. And she lost the game shortly thereafter.

She thought of that remark often now, walking to school every morning. Helping children out of their boots, scraping Play-Doh from under their nails, plastering Band-Aids onto their knees. Helping them back into their boots.

She has. No. Plan.

LUNCH WAS NOODLES with tomato sauce. As usual, Kate headed one table and Mrs. Chauncey the other, on the other side of the lunchroom, with the class divided between them. Before the children took their seats they had to hold up their hands, fronts first and then backs, for Kate or Mrs. Chauncey to inspect. Then they all sat down and Mrs. Chauncey dinged her milk glass with her fork and called out, "Blessing time!" The children ducked their heads. "Dear Lord," Mrs. Chauncey said in a ringing voice, "thank you for the gift of this food and for these fresh sweet faces. Amen."

The children at Kate's table bobbed up instantly. "Kate had her eyes open," Chloe told the others.

Kate said, "So? What of it, Miss Holy One?"

This made the Samson twins giggle. "Miss Holy One," David repeated to himself, as if memorizing the words for future use.

"If you open your eyes during blessing," Chloe said, "God will think you're not grateful."

"Well, I'm *not* grateful," Kate said. "I don't like pasta."

There was a shocked silence.

"How could you not like pasta?" Jason asked finally.

"It smells like wet dog," Kate told him. "Haven't you noticed?"

"Eew!" everyone said.

They lowered their faces to their plates and took a sniff.

"Right?" Kate asked.

They looked at one another.

"It does," Jason said.

"Like they put my dog Fritz in a big old crab pot and cooked him," Antwan said.

"*Eew!*"

"But the carrots seem okay," Kate said. She was beginning to be sorry she'd started this. "Go ahead and eat, everybody."

A couple of children picked up their forks. Most didn't.

Kate dipped a hand in her jeans pocket and brought forth a strip of beef jerky. She always carried beef jerky in case lunch didn't work out; she was a picky eater. She tore off a piece with her teeth and started chewing it. Luckily, none of the children liked beef jerky except for Emma W., who was plowing ahead with her pasta, so Kate didn't have to share.

"Happy Monday, boys and girls!" Mrs. Darling said, pegging up to their table on her aluminum cane. She made a point of stepping into the lunchroom at some point during each group's mealtime, and she always managed to work the day of the week into her greeting.

"Happy Monday, Mrs. Darling," the children murmured, while Kate surreptitiously shifted her mouthful of beef jerky into the pocket of her left cheek.

"Why are so few people eating?" Mrs. Darling asked. (Nothing escaped her.)

"The noodles smell like wet dog," Chloe said.

"Like what? My goodness!" Mrs. Darling pressed one wrinkled, speckled hand to her pouchy bosom. "It sounds to *me* as if you're forgetting the Something Nice rule," she said. "Children? Who can tell me what the Something Nice rule is?"

Nobody spoke.

"Jason?"

"'If you can't say something nice,'" Jason mumbled, "'don't say nothing at all.'"

"'Don't say anything at all.' That's right. Can somebody say something nice about our lunch today?"

Silence.

"Miss Kate? Can *you* say something nice?"

"Well, it's certainly . . . shiny," Kate said.

Mrs. Darling gave her a long, level look, but all she said was "All right, children. Have a good lunch." And she clomped off toward Mrs. Chauncey's table.

"It's as shiny as a shiny wet dog," Kate whispered to the children.

They went into shrieks of laughter. Mrs. Darling paused and then pivoted on her cane.

"Oh, by the way, Miss Kate," she said, "could you stop in at my office during Quiet Rest Time today?"

"Sure," Kate said.

She swallowed her mouthful of beef jerky.

The children turned to her with their eyes very large. Even four-year-olds knew that being called to the office was not a good thing.

"*We* like you," Jason told her after a moment.

"Thanks, Jason."

"When me and my brother grow up," David Samson said, "we're going to marry you."

"Well, thank you."

Then she clapped her hands and said, "Know what? Dessert today is cookie dough ice cream."

The children made little "Mm" sounds, but their expressions remained worried.

THEY HAD BARELY finished their ice cream when the five-year-olds arrived in the lunchroom doorway, tumbling all over one another and spilling out of line. Hulking, intimidating giants, they seemed to Kate from the confines of her little world, although only last year they had been her Fours. "Let's go, children!" Mrs. Chauncey called, heaving herself to her feet. "We're holding people up here. Say thank you to Mrs Washington."

"Thank you, Mrs. Washington," the children chorused. Mrs. Washington, standing by the door to the kitchen, smiled and nodded regally and wrapped her hands in her apron. (The Little People's School was very big on manners.) The Fours fell into a line of sorts and threaded out past the Fives in a shrinking, deferential way, with Kate bringing up the rear. As she passed Georgina, Room 5's assistant, she murmured, "I have to go to the office."

"Eek!" Georgina said. "Well, good luck with that." She was a pleasant-faced, rosy-cheeked young woman, hugely pregnant with her first child. *She* had never had to go to the office, Kate would bet.

In Room 4, she unlocked the supply closet to haul out the stacks of aluminum cots that the children took their naps on. She spaced them out around the room and distributed the blankets and the miniature pillows the children kept in their cubbies, as usual thwarting a plan among the four most talkative little girls to sleep all together in one corner. Ordinarily Mrs. Chauncey spent Quiet Rest Time in the faculty lounge, but today she'd returned to Room 4 after lunch, and now she settled herself at her desk and pulled a *Baltimore Sun* from her tote bag. She must have overheard Mrs. Darling summoning Kate to her office.

Liam D. said he wasn't sleepy. He said the same thing every day, and then he was the one Kate had to rouse from a deathlike stupor when it was Playground Time. She tucked his blanket underneath him on all sides the way he liked—a white flannel blanket with two yellow stripes that he still called his "blankie" if the other boys weren't near enough to hear him. Then Jilly needed her ponytail undone so the clasp wouldn't poke her in the head when she lay down. Kate slipped the clasp under Jilly's pillow and said, "Remember where it is, now, so you can find it when you get up." She would probably be back in time to remind her, but what if she were not? What if she were told to pack her things and leave? She ran her fingers through Jilly's hair to loosen it—soft brown hair with a silky feel to it, smelling of baby shampoo and crayons. She wouldn't be here to help Antwan work through his little bullying problem; she would never know how Emma B. dealt with the new sister who was coming from China in June.

It wasn't true that she hated children. At least, a few she liked okay. It was just that she didn't like *all* children, as if they were uniform members of some microphylum or something.

But she put on a breezy tone when she told Mrs. Chauncey, "Back in a jiff!"

Mrs. Chauncey just smiled at her (unsuspectingly? pityingly?) and turned a page of her newspaper.

Mrs. Darling's office was next to Room 2, where the children were so little that they slept on floor pads instead of cots because they might roll off. Their room was dimmed, she could see through the single pane of glass in the door, and an intense, purposeful hush seemed to emanate from it.

The glass in Mrs. Darling's door revealed Mrs. Darling at her desk, talking on the telephone while she leafed through a sheaf of papers. She said a quick good-bye and hung up, though, as soon as Kate knocked. "Come in," she called.

Kate walked in and dropped onto the straight-backed chair facing the desk.

"We've finally got an estimate for replacing that stained carpeting," Mrs. Darling told her.

"Huh," Kate said.

"The question, though, is *why* is it stained? Clearly there's some sort of leak, and till we figure it out there's no sense laying new carpet."

Kate had nothing to say to this, so she said nothing.

"Well," Mrs. Darling said. "But enough about that."

She aligned her papers efficiently and placed them in a folder. Then she reached for another folder. (Kate's folder? Did Kate have a folder? What on earth would be inside it?) She opened it and studied the top sheet of paper for a moment, and then she peered across at Kate over the rims of her glasses. "So," she said. "Kate. I'm wondering. How, exactly, would you assess your performance here?"

"My what?"

"Your performance at the Little People's School. Your teaching abilities."

"Oh," Kate said. "*I* don't know."

She was hoping this would qualify as an answer, but when Mrs. Darling went on gazing at her expectantly, she added, "I mean, I'm not really a teacher. I'm an assistant."

"Yes?"

"I just assist."

Mrs. Darling continued to gaze at her.

"But I guess I do okay at it," Kate said finally.

"Yes," Mrs. Darling said, "you do, for the most part."

Kate tried not to look surprised.

"I would say, in fact, that the children seem quite taken with you," Mrs. Darling said.

The words "for some mysterious reason" hung silently in the room.

"Unfortunately, I don't believe their parents feel the same way."

"Oh," Kate said.

"This issue has come up before, Kate. Do you remember?"

"Yeah, I remember."

"You and I have had some discussions about it. Some very *serious* discussions."

"Right."

"Just now it's Mr. Crosby. Jameesha's father."

"What about him?" Kate asked.

"He spoke to you on Thursday, he says." Mrs. Darling picked up the top sheet of paper and readjusted her glasses to consult it. "Thursday morning, when he brought Jameesha in to school. He told you he wanted to talk to you about Jameesha's thumb sucking."

"Finger sucking," Kate corrected her. Jameesha had a habit of sucking her two middle fingers, with her pinkie and her index finger sticking up on either side like the sign language for "I love you." Kate had seen that a few times before. Benny Mayo, last year, used to do that.

"Finger sucking; all right. He asked you to stop her whenever you caught her at it."

"I remember."

"And do you remember what you answered?"

"I said he shouldn't worry about it."

"Is that all?"

"I said she was bound to stop on her own, by and by."

"You said . . ." And here Mrs. Darling read aloud from the sheet of paper. "You said, 'Chances are she'll stop soon enough, once her fingers grow so long that she pokes both her eyes out.'"

Kate laughed. She hadn't realized she'd been so witty.

Mrs. Darling said, "How do you suppose that made Mr. Crosby feel?"

"How would *I* know how it made him feel?"

"Well, you might venture a guess," Mrs. Darling said. "But I'll just go ahead and tell you, why don't I. It made him feel that you were being . . ." She read aloud again. "'. . . flippant and disrespectful.'"

"Oh."

Mrs. Darling set the sheet of paper down. "Someday," she told Kate, "I can imagine your becoming a full-fledged teacher."

"You can?"

Kate had never noticed that this place had an actual career path. Certainly there had been no evidence of it to date.

"I can see you in charge of a classroom, once you mature," Mrs. Darling said. "But when I say 'mature,' Kate, I don't mean just getting older."

"Oh. No."

"I mean that you would need to develop some social skills. Some tact, some restraint, some diplomacy."

"Okay."

"Do you even understand what I'm talking about?"

"Tact. Restraint. Diplomacy."

Mrs. Darling studied her a moment. "Because otherwise," she said, "I can't quite picture your continuing in our little community, Kate. I'd *like* to picture it. I'd like to keep you on for the sake of your dear aunt, but you are walking on very thin ice here; I want you to know that."

"Got it," Kate said.

Mrs. Darling didn't seem reassured, but after a pause she said, "Very well, Kate. Leave the door open when you go, please."

"Sure thing, Mrs. D.," Kate told her.

"I THINK I'VE been put on probation," she told the Threes' assistant. They were standing out on the playground together, supervising the seesaws so that no one got killed.

Natalie said, "Weren't you already on probation?"

"Oh," Kate said. "Maybe you're right."

"What'd you do this time?"

"I insulted a parent."

Natalie grimaced. They all felt the same way about parents.

"It was this nutso control-freak dad," Kate said, "who keeps trying to turn his kid into Little Miss Perfect."

But just then Adam Barnes arrived with a couple of his Twos, and she dropped the subject. (She always tried to look like a nicer person than she really was when Adam was around.) "What's up?" he asked them, and Natalie said, "Oh, not a whole lot," while Kate just grinned at him foolishly and jammed her hands in her jeans pockets.

"Gregory here was hoping to go on a seesaw," Adam said. "I told him maybe one of the big guys would let him take a turn."

"Of course!" Natalie said. "Donny," she called, "could you give Gregory a little turn on the seesaw?"

She wouldn't do that for anyone but Adam. The children were supposed to be learning to wait—even the two-year-olds. Kate sent her a narrow-eyed stare, and Donny said, "But I just now got on!"

"Oh, then," Adam broke in immediately. "That wouldn't be fair, then. You don't want to be unfair to Donny, do you, Gregory?"

Gregory seemed to feel that he *did* want to be unfair. His eyes filled with tears and his chin started wobbling.

"Or, I know what!" Natalie said, in a super-enthusiastic tone. "Gregory, you can ride *with* Donny! Donny can be a big boy and share his ride with you!"

Kate felt like upchucking. She nearly went so far as to pantomime sticking a finger down her throat, but she stopped herself. Luckily, Adam wasn't looking in her direction. He was lifting Gregory onto the seesaw in front of Donny, who at least was tolerating the arrangement, and then he walked over to set a hand behind Jason at the other end to add some weight.

Adam was the school's only male assistant, a lanky, kind-faced young English-major type with a tangle of dark hair and a curly beard. Mrs. Darling seemed to feel she'd been exceptionally daring to have hired him, although most of the other preschools had several men on their staffs by that time. She had first assigned him to the Fives, known also as the Pre-Ks because the children there, mostly boys, were old enough for kindergarten but were thought to need a further year of socialization. A man would provide discipline and structure, Mrs. D. felt. However, Adam had turned out to be such a mild man, so gentle and solicitous, that halfway through his first year he and Georgina had been switched. Now he happily tended two-year-olds, wiping noses and soothing random cases of homesickness, and before Quiet Rest Time every day his mumbly, slightly furry voice could be heard singing lullabies above the soporific strumming of his guitar. Unlike most men, he stood noticeably taller than Kate, and yet somehow in his presence she always felt too big and too gangling. She longed all at once to be softer, daintier, more ladylike, and she was embarrassed by her own gracelessness.

She wished she had had a mother. Well, she *had* had a mother, but she wished she'd had one who had taught her how to get along in the world better.

"I saw you walk past during Quiet Rest Time," Adam called to her as he worked the seesaw. "Were you in trouble with Mrs. Darling?"

"No . . ." she said. "*You* know. We were just discussing a child I was concerned about."

Natalie made a snorting noise. Kate glared at her, and Natalie put on an exaggerated "Oh-excuse-*me*" expression. So transparent, Natalie was. Everybody knew she had a huge crush on Adam.

Last week, it was all over the school that Adam had given Sophia Watson one of his handmade dream catchers. "Oho!" everyone said. But Kate thought he might just have done that because Sophia was his co-assistant in Room 2.

TACT, RESTRAINT, DIPLOMACY. What was the difference between tact and diplomacy? Maybe "tact" referred to saying things politely while "diplomacy" meant not saying things at all. Except, wouldn't "restraint" cover that? Wouldn't "restraint" cover all three?

People tended to be very spendthrift with their language, Kate had noticed. They used a lot more words than they needed to.

She was taking her time walking home because the weather was so nice. In the morning it had been downright cold, but since then the day had warmed up and she carried her jacket slung over one shoulder. A young couple was strolling at a leisurely pace in front of her, the girl telling some long tale about some other girl named Lindy, but Kate didn't bother trying to pass them.

She wondered whether the pale blue, faceless pansies she saw in somebody's garden urn would bloom in her backyard. She had way too much shade in her backyard.

Behind her, she heard her name called. She turned

to see a light-haired man hurrying toward her with one arm raised, as if he were hailing a cab. For a moment she couldn't imagine what he had to do with her, but then she recognized her father's research assistant. The absence of his lab coat had confused her; he was wearing jeans and a plain gray jersey. "Hi!" he said as he arrived next to her. ("Khai," it sounded like.)

"Peter," she said.

"Pyotr."

"How're you doing," she said.

"I fear I may be having cold," he told her. "My nose waters and I sneeze a great deal. Has been taking place since last night."

"Bummer," she said.

She resumed walking, and he fell into step alongside her. "It was a good day at your school?" he asked.

"It was okay."

They were right on the heels of the young couple now. Lindy ought to just dump the guy, the girl was saying, he was making her unhappy; and the boy said, "Oh, I don't know, she seems all right to me."

"Where are your *eyes*?" the girl asked him. "The whole time they're together she keeps looking into his face and he keeps looking away. Everybody's noticed it—Patsy and Paula and Jane Ann—and finally my sister came right out and *said* to Lindy; she said—"

Pyotr briefly clamped Kate's upper arm to steer her around them. It startled her for a moment. He was barely taller than Kate, but she had trouble matching his stride, and then she wondered why she was trying and she slowed her pace. He slowed too. "Shouldn't you be at work?" she asked him.

"Yes! I am just going."

Since the lab lay two blocks in the opposite direction, this didn't make any sense, but that was no concern of hers. She glanced at her watch. She liked to get home before Bunny, who was not supposed to entertain boys when she was alone but sometimes did anyhow.

"In my country we have proverb," Pyotr was saying.

Didn't they always, Kate thought.

"We say, 'Work when it is divided into segments is shorter total period of time than work when it is all together in one unit.'"

"Catchy," Kate said.

"How long you have been letting your hair grow?"

The change of subject took her aback. "What?" she said. "Oh. Since eighth grade, maybe. I don't know. I just couldn't take any more of that Chatty Cathy act."

"Chatty Cathy?"

"In the beauty parlor. Talk, talk, talk; those places are *crawling* with talk. The women there start going before they even sit down—talk about boyfriends, husbands, mothers-in-law. Roommates, jealous girlfriends. Feuds and misunderstandings and romances and divorces. How can they find so much to say? I could never think of anything, myself. I kept disappointing my beautician. Finally I went, 'Shoot. I'll just quit getting my hair cut.'"

"It is exceedingly attractive," Pyotr said.

"Thanks," Kate said. "Well, this is where I turn off. Do you realize the lab's back that way?"

"Oh! Is back that way!" Pyotr said. He didn't seem too perturbed about it. "Okay, Kate! See you soon! Was nice having a talk."

Kate had already started down her own street, and she raised an arm without looking back.

SHE HAD BARELY stepped into the house when she heard a distinct male voice. "*Bunny*," she called in her sternest tone.

"In here!" Bunny sang out.

Kate tossed her jacket onto the hall bench and went into the living room. Bunny was sitting on the couch, all frothy golden curls and oh-so-innocent face and off-the-shoulder blouse far too lightweight for the season; and the Mintz boy from next door was sitting next to her.

This was a new development. Edward Mintz was several years older than Bunny, an unhealthy-looking young man with patchy beige chin whiskers that reminded Kate of lichen. He had graduated from high school two Junes ago but failed to leave for college; his mother claimed he had "that Japanese disease." "What disease is that?" Kate had asked, and Mrs. Mintz said, "The one where young people shut themselves in their bedrooms and refuse to go on with their lives." Except that Edward seemed bound not to his bedroom but to the glassed-in porch that faced the Battistas' dining-room window, where day in and day out he could be seen sitting on a chaise longue hugging his knees and smoking suspiciously tiny cigarettes.

Well, all right: no danger of romance, at least. (Bunny's weakness was football types.) Still, a rule was a rule, so Kate said, "Bunny, you know you're not supposed to entertain when you're on your own."

"Entertain!" Bunny cried, making her eyes very round and bewildered. She held up a spiral notebook that lay open on her lap. "I'm having my Spanish lesson!"

"You are?"

"I asked Papa, remember? Señora McGillicuddy said I needed a tutor? And I asked Papa and he said fine?"

"Yes, but . . ." Kate began.

Yes, but he surely hadn't meant some pothead neighbor boy. Kate didn't say this, however. (Diplomacy.) Instead, she turned to Edward and asked, "Are you especially fluent in Spanish, Edward?"

"Yes, ma'am, I had five semesters," he said. She didn't know whether the "ma'am" was smart-aleck or serious. Either way, it was annoying; she wasn't *that* old. He said, "Sometimes, I even think in Spanish."

This made Bunny give a little giggle. Bunny giggled at everything. "He's already taught me so much?" she said.

Another irksome habit of hers was turning declarative sentences into questions. Kate liked to needle her by pretending she thought they really *were* questions, so she said, "I wouldn't know that, would I, because I haven't been in the house with you."

Edward said, "What?" and Bunny told him, "Just ignore her?"

"I got an A or A-minus in Spanish every semester," Edward said, "except for senior year, and that one wasn't my fault. I was undergoing some stress."

"Well, still," Kate said, "Bunny's not allowed to have male visitors when no one else is home."

"Oh! This is *humiliating*!" Bunny cried.

"Tough luck," Kate told her. "Carry on; I'll be nearby." And she walked out.

Behind her, she heard Bunny murmur, "*Un bitcho.*"

"*Una bitch-AH*," Edward corrected her in a didactic tone.

They fell into a little spasm of snickers.

Bunny was not nearly as sweet as other people thought she was.

Kate had never quite understood why Bunny existed, even. Their mother—a frail, muted, pink-and-gold blonde with Bunny's same asterisk eyes—had spent the first fourteen years of Kate's life checking in and out of various "rest facilities," as they were called. Then all at once, Bunny was born. It was hard for Kate to imagine how her parents had considered this to be a good idea. Maybe they hadn't considered; maybe it had been a case of mindless passion. But that was even harder to imagine. At any rate, the second pregnancy had brought to light some defect in Thea Battista's heart, or perhaps had caused the defect, and she was dead before Bunny's first birthday. For Kate, it was hardly a change from the absence she'd known all her life. And Bunny didn't even remember their mother, although some of Bunny's gestures were uncannily similar—the demure tuck of her chin, for instance, and her habit of nibbling prettily on the very tip of her index finger. It was almost as if she had been studying their mother from inside the womb. Their aunt Thelma, Thea's sister, was always saying, "Oh, Bunny, I swear, it makes me cry to see you. If you aren't the image of your poor mother!"

Kate, on the other hand, was not in the least like their mother. Kate was dark-skinned and big-boned and gawky. She would have looked absurd gnawing on a finger, and nobody had ever called her sweet.

Kate was *una bitcha*.

"KATHERINE, MY DEAR!"

Kate turned from the stove, startled. Her father stood in the doorway with a shiny smile on his face. "How was your day?" he asked her.

"It was all right."

"Things went well?"

"Semi-okay."

"Excellent!" He continued standing there. As a rule, he returned from his lab in a funk, his mind still occupied with whatever he had been working on, but maybe today he'd had a breakthrough of some sort. "You walked to work, I guess," he said.

"Well, sure," she said. She always walked, unless the weather was truly miserable.

"And you had a nice walk home?"

"Yup," she said. "I ran into your assistant, by the way."

"*Did* you!"

"Yup."

"Wonderful! How was he?"

"How *was* he?" Kate repeated. "Don't *you* know how he was?"

"I mean, what did you talk about?"

She tried to remember. "Hair?" she said.

"Ah." He went on smiling. "What else?" he asked finally.

"That was it, I guess."

She turned back to the stove. She was reheating the concoction they had for supper every night. Meat mash, they called it, but it was mainly dried beans and green vegetables and potatoes, which she mixed with a small amount of stewed beef every Saturday afternoon and puréed into a grayish sort of paste to be served throughout the week. Her father was the one who had invented it. He couldn't understand why everybody didn't follow the same system; it provided all the requisite nutrients and saved so much time and decision-making.

"Father," she said, lowering the gas flame, "did you know Bunny's arranged for Edward Mintz to be her Spanish tutor?"

"Who is Edward Mintz?"

"Edward next door, Father. He was over here this afternoon when I got home from work. Here in the house, incidentally, which you'll recall is against the rules. And we have no idea if he's any good as a tutor. I don't even know what she told him we would pay him. Did she ask *you* about this?"

"Well, I believe she . . . yes, I seem to recollect she said she wasn't doing well in Spanish."

"Yes, and you said she should go ahead and find a tutor, but why didn't she get in touch with that place that's supplying her math tutor and her English tutor? Why did she hire a neighbor boy?"

"She must have had good reason," her father said.

"I don't know why you assume that," Kate told him. She banged her spoon against the side of the pot to dislodge the clump of mash that was stuck to it.

It always amazed her to see how ignorant her father was about normal everyday life. The man existed in a vacuum. Their housekeeper used to say it was because he was so smart. "He has very important matters on his mind," she would say. "Wiping out worldwide disease and such."

"Well, that shouldn't mean he can't have us on his mind besides," Kate had said. "It's like those mice of his matter more to him than we do. Like he doesn't even care about us!"

"Oh, he does, honey! He does. He just can't show it. It's like he . . . never learned the language, or something; like he comes from another planet. But I promise you he cares about you."

Their housekeeper would have thoroughly approved of Mrs. Darling's Something Nice rule.

"When I mentioned Pyoder's visa the other day," her

father was saying, "I'm not sure you fully understood the problem. His visa is good for three years. He's been here two years and ten months."

"Gee," Kate said. She turned off the burner and picked up the pot by both handles. "Excuse me."

He backed out of the doorway. She walked past him into the dining room, where she set the pot on the trivet that waited permanently in the center of the table.

Although the dining room was decorated with formal, genteel furniture handed down by Thea's ancestors, it had taken on a haphazard appearance after her death. Vitamin bottles and opened mail and various office supplies crowded the silver service on the sideboard. The unset end of the table bore a stack of receipts and a calculator and a budget book and a sheaf of income-tax forms. It always fell to Kate to do the taxes, and now she glanced guiltily at her father, who had followed on her heels. (They were perilously close to tax day.) But he was intent on his own line of thought. "You see the difficulty," he said. He followed her back to the kitchen. She took a carton of yogurt from the fridge. "Excuse me," she said again. He followed her into the dining room again. He had both fists balled up in the deep front pockets of his coveralls, which made it seem as if he were carrying a muff. "In two more months he'll be forced to leave the country," he said.

"Can't you get his visa renewed?"

"Theoretically, I can. But it's all about who's applying for him—whether that person's project is important enough, and I suspect that some of my colleagues think mine has gone off the deep end. Well, what do *they* know, right? I'm on to something here, I really feel it; I'm about to discover one single, unified key to autoimmune disorders. Still, Immigration's going to say I should just get along without him. Ever since nine-eleven, Immigration's been so unreasonable."

"Huh," Kate said. They were back in the kitchen. She chose three apples from the bowl on the counter. "So who will you get instead?"

"Instead!" her father said. He stared at her. "Kate," he said. "This is Pyoder Cherbakov! Now that I've worked with Pyoder Cherbakov, nobody else will do."

"Well, it sounds to me as if somebody else will *have* to do," Kate said. "Excuse me," she said again. She returned to the dining room, with her father once more following, and placed an apple above each plate.

"I'm ruined," her father said. "I'm doomed. I might as well abandon my research."

"Heavens, Father."

"Unless, perhaps, we could get him an . . . adjustment of status."

"Oh, good. Get him an adjustment of status."

She brushed past him and went out to the hall. "Bunny!" she shouted up the stairs. "Supper's on!"

"We could adjust his status to 'married to an American.'"

"Pyotr's married to an American?"

"Well, not quite yet," her father said. He trailed her back to the dining room. "But he's fairly nice-looking, I believe. Don't you agree? All those girls working in the building: they seem to find different reasons to talk to him."

"So could he marry a girl in the building?" Kate asked. She sat down at her place and shook out her napkin.

"I don't think so," her father said. "He doesn't . . . the conversations never seem to develop any further, unfortunately."

"Then who?"

Her father sat down at the head of the table. He cleared his throat. He said, "You, maybe?"

"Very funny," she told him. "Oh, where *is* that girl? Bernice Battista!" she shouted. "Get down here this instant!"

"I *am* down," Bunny said, arriving in the doorway. "You don't have to blast my ears off."

She plopped herself in the chair across from Kate. "Hi, Poppy," she said.

There was a long silence, during which Dr. Battista seemed to be dragging himself up from the depths. Finally he said, "Hello, Bunny." His voice had a mournful, hollow sound.

Bunny raised her eyebrows at Kate. Kate shrugged and picked up the serving spoon.

CHAPTER THREE

"HAPPY TUESDAY, CHILDREN," MRS. DARLING SAID, and then she asked Kate to come to her office again.

This time Kate couldn't leave her class during Quiet Rest Time, because Mrs. Chauncey was out sick. And on Tuesdays she was responsible for Extended Daycare once school was over. So she would be forced to stay in suspense from lunchtime until 5:30.

She didn't have the slightest idea what Mrs. Darling wanted to see her about. But then, she seldom did. The etiquette in this place was so mysterious! Or the customs, or the conventions, or whatever . . . Like not showing strangers the soles of your feet or something. She tried to cast her mind back over anything she might have done wrong, but how much *could* she have done wrong between yesterday afternoon and noon today? She had made a point of keeping her interactions with parents to a minimum, and she didn't think Mrs. Darling could have heard about her little tantrum this morning when she couldn't get Antwan's jacket unzipped. "Stupid goddamn-to-hell frigging modern *life*," she had muttered. But it was life she was cursing, not Antwan, and surely he'd understood that. Besides, he didn't seem like the kind of kid who'd go running off to tattle on people, even if he'd had the opportunity.

It had been one of those double-type zippers that could be opened from the bottom while the top stayed closed, and she'd ended up having to take the jacket off by yanking it over his head. She detested that kind of zipper. It was a presumptuous zipper; it wanted to figure out your every possible need without your say-so.

She tried to remember how Mrs. Darling had worded her threat from the day before. She hadn't said anything about "Just one more offense and you're out," had she? No, it had been less specific than that. It had been something like the vague "or else" that grown-ups were always threatening children with, that children eventually realized was not as dire as it sounded.

The phrase "thin ice" had been involved, she seemed to recollect.

How would she fill her days if she had no job anymore? There was absolutely nothing else whatsoever in her life—no reason she could think of to get out of bed every morning.

Yesterday at Show and Tell, Chloe Smith had talked about a visit she'd paid to a petting farm over the weekend. She had seen some baby goats, she said, and Kate had said, "Lucky!" (She had a soft spot for goats.) She asked, "Were they doing that frolicking thing that goats do when they're happy?"

"Yes, a few of them were just barely beginning to fly," Chloe said, and it had been such a matter-of-fact description, so concrete and unsurprised, that Kate had experienced a jolt of pure pleasure.

Funny how you have to picture losing a thing before you think you might value it after all.

At 5:40, the very last mother collected the very last child—a Room 5 mother, Mrs. Amherst, late for her son's whole career here—and Kate had given her very last fake smile, rigidly tight-lipped so that no unfortunate words could escape her. She squared her shoulders and took a deep breath and headed to Mrs. Darling's office.

Mrs. Darling was watering her houseplants. She had probably used up all other ways of killing time. Kate hoped she hadn't let boredom turn her irritable, as it would have Kate herself if she had been the one waiting, so she began by saying, "I am really, really sorry I'm late. It was Mrs. Amherst's fault."

Mrs. Darling seemed uninterested in Mrs. Amherst. "Have a seat," she told Kate, smoothing her skirt beneath her as she settled behind her desk.

Kate sat.

"Emma Gray," Mrs. Darling said. She was certainly wasting no words today.

Emma Gray? Kate's brain went racing through possibilities. There were none at all, as far as she knew. Emma Gray had never been a problem.

"Emma asked who you thought Room Four's best drawer was," Mrs. Darling said. She was consulting the notepad she kept beside her telephone. "You said"—and she read off the words—"'I think probably Jason.'"

"Right," Kate said.

She waited for the punch line, but Mrs. Darling put down her notepad as if she thought she'd already delivered it. She laced her fingers together and surveyed Kate with a "So there!" expression on her face.

"That's exactly right," Kate expanded.

"Emma's mother is very upset," Mrs. Darling told her. "She says you made Emma feel inferior."

"She *is* inferior," Kate said. "Emma G. can't draw worth a damn. She asked my honest opinion and I gave her an honest answer."

"Kate," Mrs. Darling said, "there is so much to argue with in that, I don't even know where to begin."

"What's wrong with it? I don't get it."

"Well, one thing you might have said is, 'Oh, now, Emma, I've never looked at art as a competition. I'm just so thrilled that *all* of you are creative!' you'd say. 'All of you doing your best at whatever you're trying to do.'"

Kate tried to imagine herself speaking this way. She couldn't. She said, "But Emma didn't mind; I swear she didn't. All she said was, 'Oh, yeah, Jason,' and then she went on about her business."

"She minded enough to report it to her mother," Mrs. Darling said.

"Maybe she was only making conversation."

"Children don't 'make conversation,' Kate."

In Kate's experience, making conversation was one of their favorite activities, but she said, "Well, anyhow, that happened way last week."

"And your point is?"

Kate's usual response to this question was, "Well, *gee*. Too bad you missed it." But she stifled it this time. (The unsatisfying thing about practicing restraint was that nobody knew you were practicing it.)

"So I didn't just now do it, is my point," she said. "It happened before that business with Jameesha's father, even. Before I promised to mend my ways. I mean, I remember what I promised, and I'm working on it. I'm being very diplomatic and tactful."

"I'm glad to hear it," Mrs. Darling said.

She didn't look convinced. But neither did she tell Kate she was fired. She just shook her head and said that that would be all, she supposed.

WHEN KATE ARRIVED home, she found Bunny making a mess in the kitchen. She was frying a block of something white at way too high a temperature, and the whole house had the Chinese-restaurant smell of overheated oil and soy sauce. "What *is* that?" Kate demanded, swooping past her to lower the flame.

Bunny backed away. "Don't get all in a snit, for God's sake," she said. She held up the spatula like a flyswatter. "It's tofu?"

"Tofu!"

"I'm turning vegetarian?"

"You're kidding," Kate said.

"Every hour of every day in this country, six hundred and sixty thousand innocent animals die for us."

"How do you know that?"

"Edward told me."

"Edward Mintz?"

"He doesn't eat things that have faces? So starting next week, I need you to make our meat mash without any beef."

"You want meatless meat mash."

"It would be healthier, too. You have no idea, the toxins we're stuffing our bodies with."

"Why not just join a cult?" Kate asked her.

"I knew you wouldn't understand!"

"Oh, go set the table," Kate said wearily. And she opened the fridge and took out the pot of meat mash.

Bunny hadn't always been so silly. It seemed that starting around age twelve, she had turned into a flibbertigibbet. Even her hair reflected the change. Once bound in two sensible braids, now it was a mass of springy short golden ringlets through which you could see daylight, if you stood at the proper angle. She had a habit of keeping her lips slightly parted and her eyes wide and artless, and her clothes were oddly young for her, with waistbands up under her armpits and short, short skirts prinked out around her thighs. It was all to do with boys, Kate supposed—attracting boys; except why should childishness be considered alluring to adolescent boys? (Although evidently it was. Bunny was in great demand.) In public she walked pigeon-toed, most often nibbling that fingertip, which gave her an air of timidity that could not have been more misleading. In private, though, here in the kitchen, she still walked normally. She stomped off to the dining room with an armload of plates and she slammed them down on the table one-two-three.

Kate was collecting apples from the bowl on the counter when she heard her father in the front hall. "I'll just let Kate know we're here," he was saying, and then, "Kate?" he called.

"What."

"It's us."

She exchanged a look with Bunny, who was sliding the block of tofu onto a plate now.

"Who's us?" she called.

Dr. Battista appeared in the kitchen doorway. Pyotr Shcherbakov was at his elbow.

"Oh. Pyotr," she said.

"Khello!" Pyotr said. He was wearing the same gray jersey he'd worn yesterday, and in one hand he carried a small paper bag.

"And here's my other daughter, Bunny," Dr. Battista said. "Bun-Buns, meet Pyoder."

"Hi, there! How're you doing?" Bunny asked, dimpling at him.

"For two days now I am coughing and sneezing," Pyotr told her. "Also blowing nose. Is some sort of microbe, I am thinking."

"Oh, poor you!"

"Pyoder is going to eat with us," Dr. Battista announced.

Kate said, "He is?"

She would have reminded her father that as a rule,

people informed the cook about such things ahead of time, but the fact was that in this house there *was* no rule; the situation had never come up before. The Battistas hadn't had a dinner guest for as long as Kate could remember. And Bunny was already saying, "Goody!" (Bunny was the kind of person who thought the more people, the merrier.) She pulled another clean plate from the dishwasher and another handful of silverware. Pyotr, meanwhile, held his paper bag out to Kate. "Is guest gift," he told her. "Dessert."

She took the bag from him and peered down into it. Inside were four bars of chocolate. "Well, thanks," she said.

"Ninety percent cacao. Flavonoids. Polyphenols."

"Pyoder's a big believer in dark chocolate," Dr Battista said.

"Oh, I adore chocolate!" Bunny told Pyotr. "I'm, like, addicted? I can't get enough?"

It was lucky Bunny had gone into her bubbling-over act, because Kate wasn't feeling all that hospitable herself. She took a fourth apple from the bowl and went off to the dining room, throwing her father a sour look as she passed him. He smiled and rubbed his hands together. "A little company!" he told her in a confiding voice.

"Hmph."

By the time she returned to the kitchen, Bunny was asking Pyotr what he missed most about home. She was looking up into his face with her eyes all starry and entranced, still holding the extra plate and the silverware, cocking her head encouragingly like Miss Hostess of the Month.

"I miss the pickles," Pyotr said without hesitation.

"That's so fascinating?"

"Finish setting the table," Kate told her. "Supper's ready to go, here."

"What? Wait," Dr. Battista said. "I thought we could have drinks first."

"Drinks!"

"Drinks in the living room."

"Yes!" Bunny said. "Can I have a drink, Poppy? Just a teeny-weeny glass of wine?"

"No, you cannot," Kate told her. "Your brain development's stunted enough as it is."

Pyotr gave one of his hoots. Bunny said, "Poppy! Did you hear what she said to me?"

"I meant it, too," Kate told her. "We can't afford any more tutors. Besides, Father, I'm starving to death. You were even later than usual."

"All right, all right," he said. "Sorry, Pyoder. The cook calls the shots, I guess."

"Is no problem," Pyotr said.

This was just as well, because as far as Kate knew, the only alcohol in the house was an open bottle of Chianti from last New Year's.

She carried the meat mash into the dining room and put it on the trivet. Bunny, meanwhile, set a place for Pyotr next to her own; they all had to crowd at one end because of the income-tax papers. "How about people,

Pyoder?" she asked him once he was settled. (The girl was tireless.) "Don't you miss any *people* from home?"

"I have no people," he said.

"None at all?"

"I grew up in orphanage."

"Gosh! I never met anybody from an orphanage before!"

"You forgot Pyotr's water," Kate told her. She was dishing out mounds of meat mash and passing the filled plates around, exchanging them for empty ones.

Bunny pushed her chair back and started to rise, but Pyotr held a palm up and said again, "Is no problem."

"Pyoder feels water dilutes the enzymes," Dr Battista said.

Bunny said, "Huh?"

"The digestive enzymes."

"Especially water with ice," Pyotr said. "Freezes enzymes in middle of ducts."

"Have you ever heard this theory?" Dr. Battista asked his daughters. He looked delighted.

Kate thought it was a pity he couldn't just marry Pyotr himself, if he was so set on adjusting the man's status. The two of them seemed made for each other.

On Tuesdays, Kate varied their menu by setting out tortillas and a jar of salsa so that they could have meat-mash burritos. Pyotr didn't bother with the tortillas, though. He ladled an avalanche of salsa over his serving and then dug in with his spoon, nodding intently as he listened to Dr. Battista ponder why it was that auto-immune disorders affected more women than men. Kate pushed her food around her plate; she wasn't as hungry as she had thought. And Bunny, across the table from her, seemed lukewarm about her tofu. She cut a corner off with her fork and took an experimental taste, chewing with just her front teeth. Her green vegetable—two pallid stalks of celery—lay untouched, so far. Kate predicted her meat-free phase would last about three days.

Dr. Battista was telling Pyotr that sometimes it seemed to him that women were just more . . . skinless than men, but he stopped speaking suddenly and looked at Bunny's plate. "What's that?" he asked.

"It's tofu?"

"Tofu!"

"I've given up eating meat?"

"Is that wise?" her father asked.

"Is ridiculous," Pyotr said.

"See there?" Kate told Bunny.

"Where would be her B-twelve?" Pyotr asked Dr. Battista.

"I suppose it could come from her breakfast cereal," Dr. Battista mused. "Providing the cereal's fortified, of course."

"Is still ridiculous," Pyotr said. "Is so American, subtracting foods! Other countries, when they want healthiness they add foods in. Americans subtract them."

Bunny said, "How about, like, canned tuna? That doesn't have a face per se. Could I get B-twelve from canned tuna?"

Kate was so surprised at Bunny's tossing off that "per se" that it took her a moment to realize their father was way, way overreacting to the suggestion of tuna. He was holding his head in both hands and rocking back and forth. "No, no, *no*, no, no!" he groaned.

They all stared at him.

He raised his head and said, "Mercury."

"Ah," Pyotr said.

Bunny said, "Well, I don't care; I refuse to eat little baby calves that are kept in cages all their lives and never touch their feet to the ground."

"You are so far off topic," Kate told her. "That's veal you're talking about! I never put veal in meat mash!"

"Veal, beef, soft woolly lambs . . ." Bunny said. "I don't want any of them. It's wicked. Tell me, Pyoder," she said, wheeling on him, "how can you live with yourself, making little mousies suffer?"

"Mousies?"

"Or whatever animals you're torturing over there in that lab."

"Oh, Bun-Buns," Dr. Battista said sorrowfully.

"I do not torture mice," Pyotr said with dignity. "They live very good lives in your father's lab. Recreation! Companionship! Some of them have names. They live better than in outdoors."

"Except that you stick them with needles," Bunny said.

"Yes, but—"

"And those needles make them sick."

"No, at current time they do *not* make them sick, which is interesting, you see, because—"

The telephone rang. Bunny said, "I'll get it!"

She scraped back her chair and jumped up and ran to the kitchen, leaving Pyotr sitting there with his mouth open.

"Hello?" Bunny said. "Oh, hi-yee! Hi, there!"

Kate could tell it was a boy she was talking to because of the breathy, shallow voice she put on. Amazingly, their father seemed able to sense it too. He frowned and said, "Who *is* that?" Then he turned and called, "Bunny? Who is that?"

Bunny ignored him. "Aww," they heard her say. "Aww, that's so sweet! Aren't you sweet to say so!"

"Who is she talking to?" Dr. Battista asked Kate.

She shrugged.

"It's bad enough when she gets those . . . *textings* all meal long," he said. "Now they're calling her on the phone?"

"Don't look at *me*," Kate told him.

Kate would have choked on her own words, talking like that on the phone. She would have lost all self-respect. She tried to imagine it for a moment: getting a call from, oh, maybe Adam Barnes and telling him he was so sweet to say whatever he said to her. The very thought of it made her toes curl.

"Did you speak to her about the Mintz boy?" she asked her father.

"What Mintz boy?"

"Her tutor, Father."

"Oh. Not yet."

She sighed and offered Pyotr another helping of meat mash.

❧

PYOTR AND DR. BATTISTA fell into a discussion involving lymphoproliferation. Bunny returned from her phone call and sat pouting between them and cutting her block of tofu into infinitesimal cubes. (She wasn't used to being ignored.) At the end of the meal Kate rose and brought in the chocolate bars from the kitchen, but she didn't bother clearing the plates and so everyone just dropped the wrappers on top of the remains of dinner.

After Kate's first bite of chocolate she grimaced; ninety percent cacao was about thirty percent too much, she decided. Pyotr looked amused. "In my country, is a proverb," he told her. "'If the medication does not taste bitter, then it will fail to cause effective cure.'"

"I'm not used to expecting a cure from my desserts," she said.

"Well, *I* think it tastes excellent," Dr. Battista said. He probably didn't realize that his lips were pulled down at the corners like a Room 4 drawing of a frowny face. Bunny didn't seem too pleased with the chocolate either, but then she jumped up and went out to the kitchen and returned with a jar of honey.

"Put some of this on," she told Kate.

Kate waved it away and reached for the apple at the head of her plate.

"Poppy? Put some of this on."

"Why, thank you, Bunnikins," her father said. He dipped a corner of his chocolate bar into the jar. "Honey from Bunny."

Kate rolled her eyes.

"Honey is one of my favorite nutraceuticals," her father told Pyotr.

Bunny offered the jar to Pyotr. "Pyoder?" she asked.

"I am okay."

He was watching Kate, for some reason. He had a way of keeping his lids at half-mast, which made him seem to be arriving at some private conclusion as he studied her.

There was a loud clicking sound. Kate started and turned toward her father, who waved his cell phone at her. "I think I'm getting the hang of this thing," he said.

"Well, quit it."

"I only wanted to practice."

"Take one of me," Bunny begged. She put her chocolate bar down and dabbed her mouth hastily with her napkin. "Take one and send it to my phone."

"I don't know how to do that yet," her father said. But he snapped her picture anyhow. Then he said, "Pyoder, you were hidden behind Bunny in that one. Go over and sit next to Kate and let me take one of both of you."

Pyotr promptly changed places, but Kate said, "What's got into you, Father? You've had that phone a year and a half and you never gave it a glance until now."

"It's time I joined the modern world," he told her, and he raised the phone to his eye again as if it were a Kodak. Kate pushed her chair back and stood up, trying to get out of the shot, and the click sounded again and her father lowered the phone to check the results.

"I shall help wash the dishes," Pyotr told Kate. He stood up too.

"Never mind; that's Bunny's job."

"Oh, tonight why don't you and Pyoder do it," Dr. Battista said, "because Bunny has homework, I'll bet."

"No, I don't," Bunny said.

Bunny almost never had homework. It was mystifying.

"Well, but we need to talk about your math tutor, though," Dr. Battista said.

"What about her?"

"Spanish tutor," Kate said.

"We need to talk about your Spanish tutor. Come along," he said, standing.

"I don't know what we need to say about him," Bunny told her father, but she rose and followed him out of the room.

Pyotr was already stacking plates. Kate said, "Seriously, Pyotr, I've got this under control. Thanks anyhow."

"You say this because I am foreign," he told her, "but I know that American men wash dishes."

"Not in this house. Actually, none of us do. We just throw them in the machine and run it whenever it's full. We take some out for the next meal, and then we put them back in and run the machine when it's full again."

He thought about it. "This means some dishes are washed two times," he said, "even though they were not eaten from."

"Two times or half a dozen times; you got it."

"And sometimes you are maybe using already eaten-from dish, by accident."

"Only if one of us has licked it really, really clean," she said. She laughed. "It's a system. Father's system."

"Ah, yes," he said. "A system."

He turned on the faucet in the sink and started rinsing plates. Her father's system did not involve pre-rinsing; just send any scuzzy dish through the machine a second time, were his instructions. Besides, even without the second pass they would know it had at least been sterilized. But she sensed that Pyotr already disapproved enough and so she didn't try to stop him.

Although he was running hot water, which was terrible for the environment and would have driven her father crazy.

"There is no housemaid?" Pyotr asked after a moment.

"Not anymore," Kate said. She was putting the meat mash back in the fridge. "That's why we have Father's systems."

"Your mother passed away."

"Died," Kate said. "Yep."

"I am sorry for your loss," he said. He spoke as if he'd memorized the sentence word for word.

"Oh, that's okay," Kate said. "I never knew her that well."

"Why you did not know her?"

"She developed some kind of depression right after I was born." Kate was in the dining room now, wiping off the table. She returned to the kitchen and said, "Took one look at me and fell into despair." She laughed.

Pyotr didn't laugh himself. She remembered he'd been reared in an orphanage. "I guess you didn't know *your* mother, either," she said.

"No," he said. He was slotting plates into the dish-washer. Already they looked clean enough to eat off of. "I was found."

"A foundling?"

"Yes, found on porch. In box for canned peaches. Note said only, 'Two days old.'"

When he was talking shop with her father he had sounded halfway intelligent—thoughtful, even—but on subjects less scientific his language turned stunted again. She couldn't find any logic to his use or non-use of article adjectives, for instance, and how hard could article adjectives be?

She tossed her dishcloth into the hamper in the pantry. (Her father believed in 100-percent cotton dishcloths, used once and then laundered with bleach. He viewed sponges with an almost superstitious horror.)

"Well, all done here," she told Pyotr. "Thanks for helping. Father's in the living room, I think."

He stood looking at her, perhaps waiting for her to lead the way, but she leaned back against the sink and folded her arms across her chest. Eventually, he turned and left the kitchen, and Kate went to the dining room to work on the income tax.

"THAT WENT WELL, don't you agree?" her father asked her.

He had drifted into the dining room after seeing Pyotr off. Kate totaled a column before she looked up, and then she said, "Did you talk to Bunny?"

"Bunny," he said.

"Did you talk to her about Edward Mintz?"

"I did."

"What'd she say?"

"About what?"

Kate sighed. "Let's try to concentrate, here," she said. "Did you ask her why she didn't just get a tutor from the agency? Did you find out how much money he's charging?"

"He's not charging any money."

"Well, *that's* not good."

"Why not?"

"We want this arrangement to be on a professional footing. We want to be able to fire him if he turns out to be no help."

"Would you be willing to marry Pyoder?" her father asked.

"What?"

She sat back in her chair and gaped at him, the calculator still in her left hand, the ballpoint pen in her right. The full import of his question slammed into her after several seconds' delay—a kind of thud to the midriff.

He didn't repeat it. He stood waiting trustfully for an answer, with his fists balled up in his coverall pockets.

"Please tell me you're not serious," she said.

"Now, just consider the possibility, Kate," he said. "Don't make any hasty decisions till you've given it some thought."

"You're saying you want me to marry someone I don't even know so that you can hang onto your research assistant."

"He's not any *ordinary* research assistant; he's Pyoder Cherbakov. And you *slightly* know him. And you have my word as a reference for him."

"You've been hinting at this for days, haven't you?" she asked. It was humiliating to hear how her voice shook; she hoped he didn't notice. "You've been throwing him at me all along and I was too dumb to see it. I guess I just couldn't believe my own father would conceive of such a thing."

"Now, Kate, you're overreacting," her father said. "You'll have to marry someone sooner or later, right? And this is someone so exceptional, so gifted; it would be such a loss to mankind if he had to leave my project. And I like the fellow! He's a good fellow! I'm sure you'll come to feel the same way once you're better acquainted."

"You would never ask Bunny to do this," Kate said bitterly. "Your precious treasure Bunny-poo."

"Well, Bunny's still in high school," he said.

"Let her drop out, then; it's not as if it would be any loss to the world of learning."

"Kate! That's uncharitable," her father said. "Besides," he added after a moment, "Bunny has all those young men chasing after her."

"And I don't," Kate said.

He didn't argue with that. He looked at her mutely, hopefully, with his lips tensely pursed so that his little black mustache bunched itself together.

If she kept her expression impassive, if she didn't blink or even open her mouth to say another word, she might be able to stop the tears from spilling over. So she was silent. By degrees she stood up, careful not to bump into anything, and she set down her calculator and turned and walked out of the dining room with her chin raised.

"Katherine?" her father called after her.

She reached the hall, she crossed the hall, and then she started pounding up the stairs with the tears positively streaming, flying off her cheeks as she arrived on the landing and rounded the newel post and ran smack into Bunny, who was just starting down. "Hello?" Bunny said, looking startled.

Kate threw her pen into Bunny's face and stumbled into her own room and slammed the door behind her.

CHAPTER FOUR

YOU COULD REALLY FEEL PHYSICALLY WOUNDED IF someone hurt your feelings badly enough. Over the next few days, she discovered that. She had discovered it several times before, but this felt like a brand-new revelation, as sharp as a knife to her chest. Illogical, of course: why her chest? Hearts were just glorified pumps, after all. Still, her own heart felt bruised, simultaneously shrunken and swollen, and if that sounded self-contradictory, well, so be it.

She walked to work every day feeling starkly, conspicuously alone. It seemed that everyone else on the street had someone to keep them company, someone to laugh with and confide in and nudge in the ribs. All those packs of young girls who'd already figured everything out. All those couples interlinked and whispering with their heads together, and those neighbor women gossiping next to their cars before they left for work. Eccentric husbands, impossible teenagers, star-crossed friends they gossiped about, and then they would break off and "Morning" they would say to Kate—even the ones who didn't know her. Kate pretended not to hear. If she ducked her head low enough, her hair would swing forward so it completely hid her profile.

The weather was more springlike now, and the daffodils were beginning to bloom and the birds were downright raucous. If her time had been her own, she would have worked in the garden. That always soothed her spirits. But no, she had to go to school every morning, and plaster a flashy smile on her face when she arrived at the main entrance where the parents were dropping their children off. Some of the younger children were still reluctant to say good-bye even this late in the school year, and they would cling fiercely to their parents' knees and bury their faces, and the parents would send Kate a woebegone look and Kate would put on a commiserating, entirely fraudulent expression and ask the child, whoever it was, "Want me to hold your hand while we go in?" This was because Mrs. Darling was standing in the doorway, waiting for any excuse to fire her. Although so what if she were fired? What difference would it make?

On her way to Room 4 she gave no more than a nod to any teachers or assistants she saw conversing in the corridor. She said hello to Mrs. Chauncey and she stowed her belongings in the supply closet. As the children entered the room they raced over to catch her up on some piece of urgent news—a pet's new trick, a scary dream, a present from a grandmother—and often several were speaking at once while Kate stood in their midst as still as a tree and said, "Really. Huh. Just imagine." It felt like the most tremendous effort, but none of the children seemed to notice that.

She went through the motions of Show and Tell, Story Time, Activity Hour. She took a break in the faculty lounge, where Mrs. Bower was debating cataract surgery or Mrs. Fairweather was asking whether anyone else had ever had bursitis, and they would all pause to greet her and Kate would mumble something like "Mmph" and let her curtain of hair fall forward as she proceeded to the restroom.

Room 4 seemed to be passing through a particularly contentious period, and all the little girls stopped speaking to Liam M. "What did you do to them?" Kate asked him, and he said, "I don't *know* what I did." Kate believed him, too. Sometimes very complicated machinations went on with those little girls. She told Liam M., "Well, never mind, they'll get over it by and by," and he nodded and heaved an enormous sigh and threw his shoulders back bravely.

At lunch she would stir her food listlessly around her plate; everything smelled like waxed paper. On Friday she forgot her beef jerky—or rather, she found the drawer at home empty although she could have sworn she still had some—and she didn't eat a thing except a couple of grapes, but that was okay; she felt not just lacking in appetite but overstuffed, as if that swollen heart of hers had risen in her throat.

At Quiet Rest Time she sat behind Mrs. Chauncey's desk and stared into space. Ordinarily she would have flipped through Mrs. Chauncey's discarded newspaper or tidied up some of the more clutter-prone play areas—the Lego corner or the crafts table—but now she just gazed at nothing and racked up points against her father.

He must think she was of no value; she was nothing

but a bargaining chip in his single-minded quest for a scientific miracle. After all, what real purpose did she have in her life? And she couldn't possibly find a man who would love her for herself, he must think, so why not just palm her off on someone who would be useful to him?

It wasn't that Kate had never had a boyfriend. After she graduated from high school, where the boys had seemed a little afraid of her, she'd had a *lot* of boyfriends. Or a lot of first dates, at least. Sometimes even second dates. Her father had no business giving up on her like that.

Besides, she was only twenty-nine years old. There was plenty of time to find a husband! Provided she even wanted one, and she was not so sure that she did.

Out on the playground on Friday afternoon, aimlessly kicking a bottle cap across the hard-packed earth, she tortured herself by rehashing all that her father had said to her. He liked the fellow, he'd said. As if that were sufficient reason to marry his daughter off to him! And then the part about how Pyotr's leaving the project would be such a loss to mankind. Her father didn't care the least little bit about mankind. That project had become an end in itself. To all intents and purposes, it had no end. It just went on and on, generating its own spinoffs and detours and switchbacks, and no one except other scientists even knew what it was, exactly. Recently, Kate had begun to wonder whether even other scientists knew. It seemed possible that his sponsors had forgotten he existed; that they continued funding him purely from force of habit. He'd been phased out of teaching long ago (she could just picture what kind of teacher he'd made) and stuck away in that series of steadily shrinking and peregrinating laboratories, and when Johns Hopkins established a dedicated autoimmune research center he had not been invited to join. Or maybe he had refused to join; she wasn't entirely sure. In any case, he just went on working away by himself without, apparently, anyone's bothering to investigate whether he was making any progress. Though who knew? Perhaps he was making all kinds of progress. But at this particular moment, Kate couldn't invent a single result that would justify sacrificing his firstborn.

She mistakenly kicked a tuft of grass instead of the bottle cap, and a child waiting for his turn at the swings looked startled.

Natalie might be succeeding in winning Adam's affections. She looked so pretty and poetic, crouching to console a little girl with a scraped elbow, and Adam stood next to her watching sympathetically. "Why don't you take her inside for a Band-Aid?" he asked. "I'll supervise the seesaws," and Natalie said, "Oh, would you? Thank you, Adam," and she rose in one graceful motion and shepherded the child toward the building. She was wearing a dress today, which was unusual among the assistants. It swished around her calves seductively, and Adam gazed after her longer than he needed to, it seemed to Kate.

Once, a couple of months ago, Kate had tried wearing a skirt to school herself. Not that it was swishy or anything; actually it was a denim skirt with rivets and a front zip, but she had thought it might make her seem . . . softer. The older teachers had turned all knowing and glinty. "*Somebody's* making a big effort today!" Mrs. Bower had said, and Kate had said, "What, this? It was the only thing not in the wash, is all." But Adam hadn't seemed to register its existence. Anyhow, it had proved impractical—hard to climb a jungle gym in—and she couldn't shake the image of the reflection she had glimpsed in the faculty restroom's full-length mirror. "Mutton dressed as lamb" was the phrase that had come to mind, although she knew she wasn't really mutton; not yet. The next day, she had gone back to Levi's.

Now Adam sauntered over to her and said, "Have you ever noticed that certain days are injury days?"

"Injury days?"

"That kid just now, with her elbow; and then this morning one of my boys sharpened his index finger in the pencil sharpener—"

"Ooh!" she said, wincing.

"—and just before lunch Tommy Bass knocked his front tooth out and we had to call his mother to come get him—"

"Ooh, that *is* an injury day," Kate said. "Did you put the tooth in milk?"

"In milk."

"You put it in a cup of milk and it has a chance of being re-implanted?"

"Gosh, no, I didn't," Adam said. "I just wadded it up in a Kleenex in case they wanted it for the tooth fairy."

"Well, don't worry; it was only a baby tooth."

"How do you know about the milk trick?" he asked.

"Oh, I just do," she said.

She couldn't figure out where to put her hands so she started swinging her arms back and forth from her shoulders, till she remembered that Bunny had told her she looked like a boy when she did that. (Count on Bunny.) She stopped swinging her arms and stuffed her hands in her rear pockets. "I had a grown-up tooth knocked out by a baseball when I was nine," she said. Then she realized how unfeminine that sounded and so she added, "I was just walking past a game on my way home? Was how it happened. But our housekeeper knew to put the tooth in milk."

"Well, it must have worked," Adam said, looking at her more closely. "You have great teeth."

"Oh, aren't you . . . isn't it nice of you to say so?" Kate said.

She started drawing arcs in the dirt with the toe of her sneaker. Then Sophia walked over, and she and Adam began discussing a recipe for no-knead bread.

During Afternoon Activity Hour, the ballerina doll and the sailor doll had one of their breakups. (Kate wasn't aware that they had gotten back together.) This time they were breaking up because the sailor doll had been inappropriate. "Please, Cordelia," Emma G. said, speaking for the sailor, "I'll never be inappropriate again, I promise." But the ballerina said, "Well, I'm sorry, but I have given you chance after chance and now you are walking on my last nerve." Then Jameesha fell off a stepstool and developed a giant lump on her forehead, proving Adam's point about injury days; and after Kate had managed to divert her, Chloe and Emma W. got into a shouting quarrel. "Girls! Girls!" Mrs. Chauncey said. She had a lower tolerance for discord than Kate did. Chloe said, "It's not fair! Emma W.'s hogging the child dolls! She has Drink-and-Wet and Squeaky Baby and Anatomically Correct, and all I have is this dumb old wooden Pinocchio!" Mrs. Chauncey turned toward Kate, clearly expecting her to mediate, but Kate just told them, "Well, sort it out," and walked off to see what the boys were doing. One of the boys had a doll as well (a child doll, she saw), and he was sliding it facedown along the floor and saying "*Vroom, vroom*" as if it were a truck, which seemed a waste, since child dolls were in such demand today, but Kate wasn't up to dealing with it. The wounded feeling had spread from her chest to her left shoulder, and she wondered if she were having a heart attack. She would have welcomed it.

WALKING HOME AT the end of the day, she reviewed her conversation with Adam. "Ooh!" she had said, not once but twice, in that artificial, girlie way she detested, and her voice had come out higher-pitched than usual and her sentences had slanted upward at the end. Stupid, stupid, stupid. "Isn't it nice of you to say so?" she'd asked. Mrs. Gordon's miniature Japanese maple brushed her face as she passed, and she gave it a vicious swat. As she approached the Mintzes' house their front door opened, and she speeded up so as not to have to speak to anyone.

Bunny wasn't home yet. Good. Kate slung her bag onto the hall bench and went to the kitchen for something to eat. Her stomach had begun to notice that she had skipped lunch. She cut herself a chunk of cheddar and strolled around the kitchen as she munched on it, assessing what she would need to pick up tomorrow at the grocery store. If she cooked next week's meat mash without the meat (which she had decided she would do, just to call Bunny's bluff), she would have to increase some other ingredient—the lentils, maybe, or the yellow split peas. Her father's recipe was calibrated so that they finished the dish completely on Friday evenings. But this past week had been an exception: since Bunny had turned vegetarian she had not been doing her part, and even the addition of Pyotr on Tuesday, wolfish eater though he had been, had not made up for it. They were going to be left with extras tomorrow, and her father would be unhappy.

Reluctantly, she deleted *stew beef* from the shopping list. The list was computer-generated—her father's work, the household's usual supplies arranged according to their order in the supermarket aisles—and all she had to do every week was cross off what wasn't needed. Today she crossed off the salami sticks Bunny ordinarily snacked on; she left *beef jerky* uncrossed and she added *shampoo*, which her father had not included in his prototype list because it was his opinion that a bar of plain soap would do the same job for a fraction of the price.

In the old days, when they still had their housekeeper, things had been less regimented. Not that Dr. Battista hadn't tried; Mrs. Larkin's easygoing ways used to drive him to distraction. "What's wrong with just writing down what I want whenever I think of it?" she'd asked when he'd urged his list on her. "It's not that hard: carrots, peas, chicken . . ." (Mrs. Larkin used to make a wonderful chicken potpie.) Out of his hearing, she had warned Kate not ever to let a man meddle with the housework. "He'll get all carried away with it," she'd said, "and your life won't never be your own after that."

One of Kate's few memories of her mother involved an argument that had developed when her father tried to tell her mother she was loading the dishwasher wrong. "Spoons should go in with their handles down, knives and forks with their handles up," he had said. "If you do it that way, you see, the knives and forks will never poke you, and you can sort out the silverware basket much faster when it's time to empty the dishwasher." This was before he had evolved the notion of not emptying it ever again, obviously. To Kate the plan had sounded sensible, but her mother had ended up in tears and retreated to her bedroom.

There was a clementine in the bowl on the counter, left over from a box that Kate had bought back in February. She peeled it and ate it, even though it was slightly shriveled. She stood at the sink and looked out the window at the little red birdhouse she had hung last week in the dogwood tree. So far, no birds had been interested. She knew it was silly of her to take this personally.

Was Pyotr aware of what her father had been plotting? He had to be, she supposed. (How mortifying.) He had needed to play his part, after all—"accidentally" catching up with her as she walked home that time, and making all that fuss about her hair, and then coming to dinner. Also, he hadn't looked like a man who was worried that his visa was about to expire. He'd probably been taking it for granted that her father's scheme would save him.

Well, *now* he wasn't taking anything for granted. Ha! By now he would have heard that she had refused to cooperate. She wished she could have seen his face when he found out.

You can't get around Kate Battista as easily as all that.

She carried a laundry basket upstairs and filled it with the clothes in the hamper in Bunny's room. According to their father, the most time-consuming part of doing the laundry was separating different people's clothes afterward. He had decreed that each of them should have an individual washday, and Bunny's was Friday. Although Kate, wouldn't you know, was the one who always *did* the laundry.

Bunny's bedroom had a bruised-fruit smell from all the cosmetics cluttering her bureau. A good many of the clothes that should have been in the hamper were scattered across the floor, but Kate let them stay there. Picking them up was not her job.

In the basement, something about the dusty gloom made her limbs feel heavy and achy, all at once. She set the basket down and just stood there a moment, clamping her forehead with one hand. Then she straightened and flipped up the lid of the washing machine.

❧

She was gardening when Bunny came home. She was cleaning out some of the old growth on the clematis vine beside the garage, and Bunny opened the back screen door to call, "You out there?"

Kate turned and blotted her forehead on her sleeve.

"What've we got to eat?" Bunny asked her. "I'm starved."

Kate said, "Did you take the last of my beef jerky?"

"Who, me? Do you not remember I'm a vegan?"

"You're a vegan?" Kate repeated. "Wait. You're a *vegan*?"

"Vegan, vegetarian; whatever."

Kate said, "If you don't even know which is which—"

"Is my wash done yet?"

"It's in the dryer."

"You didn't put my off-the-shoulder blouse in, did you?"

"I did if it was in the hamper."

"Kate! Honestly! You know I save my whites out for sheets day."

"If you want something saved out, you should be here to see to it," Kate said.

"I had cheerleading practice! I can't be everywhere at once!"

Kate went back to her gardening.

"This family is so lame," Bunny said. "Other people separate their colors."

Kate stuffed a snarl of vine into her trash bag.

"Other people's clothes don't come out all the same gray."

Kate wore only darks and plaids, herself. She didn't find the subject worth discussing.

AT SUPPER, HER father poured forth compliments. "Did you grind your own curry powder?" he asked. (The meat mash metamorphosed into a curry on Fridays.) "It tastes so authentic."

"Nope," she said.

"Maybe it has to do with the amount you put in, then. I really like the spiciness."

He had behaved this way for the past three days. It was pathetic.

Bunny was having a toasted cheese sandwich with a side of green-onion potato chips. She claimed the potato chips were her vegetable. Fine, let her die of scurvy. It was all the same to Kate.

The only sounds for a while were the crunching of chips and the clink of forks against plates. Then Dr. Battista cleared his throat. "So," he began delicately. "So, I notice we still have the tax papers here."

"Right," Kate said.

"Ah, yes. I only mention it because . . . it occurred to me there's a deadline."

"Really?" Kate said, raising her eyebrows in astonishment. "A deadline! Fancy that!"

"I mean . . . but probably you're already bearing that in mind, though."

Kate said, "You know what, Father? I think this year you should do your own taxes."

His mouth flew open and he stared at her.

"You do yours; I do mine," Kate said. Hers were about as simple as taxes could get, and in fact they were already finished and mailed.

Her father said, "Oh, why . . . but you're so good at them, Katherine."

"I'm sure you can figure them out," Kate said.

He turned to Bunny. Bunny gave him a bland smile. Then she looked across the table at Kate and raised a fist toward the ceiling. "Go, Katherine!" she said.

Well. Kate had not seen *that* one coming.

BUNNY WAS PICKED up by a mother driving a crowd of teenage girls who were squealing and laughing and waving wildly out all the open windows. Drumbeats pounded from the radio. "Have you got your phone?" Kate asked, and then, belatedly, "Where will you be?"

Bunny just said, "Bye-yee!" and she was out the door and gone.

Kate finished making her father's lunch for the next day, and then she turned off the lights in the kitchen and the dining room. Her father was reading in the living room. He sat in his leather armchair beneath a pool of yellow lamplight, and seemingly he was absorbed in his journal, but when Kate crossed the hall there was a certain stiffening in his posture, an *awareness*. Before he could attempt to start a conversation, though, she took a sharp left turn and climbed the stairs two at a time. She heard the creak of leather behind her, but he didn't try to stop her.

Although dusk had barely fallen, she changed into her pajamas. (It was tiring, dragging herself around all day.) She stared at herself in the bathroom mirror after she had brushed her teeth; she let her head tip forward till it was resting against the glass and she looked into her own eyes, which from this angle had bags beneath them almost as dark as her irises. Then she returned to her room and climbed into her bed. She propped her pillow against the headboard and adjusted the shade of her lamp and took her book from the nightstand and started reading.

She was reading a Stephen Jay Gould book that she had read before. She liked Stephen Jay Gould. She liked nonfiction—books about natural history or evolution. She didn't have much use for novels. Although she did enjoy a good time-travel novel, now and again. Whenever she had trouble sleeping, she fantasized about traveling back through time to the Cambrian Era. The Cambrian Era was some 450 million years ago. Just about the only living creatures then were invertebrates, and not a one of them lived on dry land.

CHAPTER FIVE

LAST FALL KATE HAD PLANTED AN ASSORTMENT OF
spring crocuses beneath the redbud tree in the backyard, and she had been on the lookout for several weeks
now but not a one had shown itself. It was puzzling. She
checked again on Saturday morning after her grocery
trip; she poked around with her trowel, even, but she
couldn't find a single bulb. Was this the work of moles, or
voles, or some other kind of varmint?

She quit digging and stood up, flinging back her
hair, just as the telephone rang in the kitchen. Bunny
was awake, she knew—earlier she'd heard the shower
running—but the telephone rang again and then again.
By the time she'd made it into the house, the answering
machine had swung into its "Hi-yee!" and then her father
was saying, "Pick up, Kate. It's your father."

Already, though, she had spotted his lunch bag on the
counter. She didn't know how she had missed it before.
She stopped just inside the back door and scowled at it
ferociously.

"Kate? Are you there? I forgot my lunch."

"Well, isn't that just too damn bad," Kate told the
empty kitchen.

"Could you bring it to me, please?"

She turned and went back outside. She tossed her trowel into her gardening bucket and reached for her dandelion weeder.

The telephone rang again.

This time, she made it into the house before the answering machine could click over. She snatched up the receiver and said, "How many times did you think I'd fall for this, Father?"

"Ah, Kate! Katherine. It seems I've forgotten my lunch again."

She was silent.

"Are you there?"

"I guess you'll have to go hungry," she said.

"Excuse me? Please, Kate. I don't ask very much of you."

"Actually, you ask a lot of me," she told him.

"I just need you to bring my lunch. I haven't eaten since last night."

She considered. Then she said, "Fine," and slammed the receiver down before she could hear his response.

She went out to the hall and shouted up the stairs: "Bunny?"

"What," Bunny said, from much nearer than Kate had expected.

Kate turned from the stairs and went to the living-room doorway. Bunny and Edward Mintz were sitting rather close together on the couch. Bunny had an open book on her lap. "Hi, there, Kate!" Edward said enthusiastically. He was wearing jeans so ragged that both of his hairy bare knees poked out.

Kate ignored him. "Father needs his lunch brought," she told Bunny.

"Brought where?"

"Where do you think? How come you didn't answer the phone when it rang?"

"Because I'm having my Spanish lesson?" Bunny said indignantly, spreading her palms to indicate her book.

"Well, take a break from it and run over to the lab."

"Your dad's in his lab on Saturdays?" Edward asked Bunny.

"He's always in his lab?" Bunny said. "He works seven days a week?"

"What, on Sundays too?"

"I don't know why *you* can't do it," Bunny told Kate, speaking over Edward's words.

"I'm gardening, is why," Kate said.

"I'll drive you there," Edward told Bunny. "Where is this lab, exactly?"

Kate said, "Sorry. Bunny's not allowed to ride alone with a boy."

"Edward's not a boy!" Bunny protested. "He's my tutor?"

"You know Father's rule. Not till you're sixteen."

"But I'm a really responsible driver," Edward told Kate.

"Sorry; it's the rule."

Bunny snapped her book shut and flung it onto the couch. "There are plenty of girls in my school a whole lot younger than me that get to ride alone with boys every night of the week," she said.

"Tell Father that; it's not *my* rule," Kate said.

"It might as well be. You're just exactly like him: two peas in a pod."

"I'm what? Take that back!" Kate said. "I'm not a bit like him!"

"Oh, so sorry, my mistake," Bunny said, with a luminous, sweet smile playing at the corners of her mouth. (The smile of all the mean girls Kate used to know in seventh grade.) She stood up and said, "Come along, Edward."

He stood up too and followed her. "I am the one and only normal person in this family," she told him. Kate trailed them through the hall. In the kitchen doorway, she had to stand aside because Bunny was already stalking back out, violently swinging the lunch bag. "The other two are crazy people," she was telling Edward. He followed her toward the front of the house like a pet dog.

Kate opened the fridge and took out a roast beef sandwich she had bought at the deli counter that morning. Already she was feeling meat-deprived, although she hadn't even assembled her vegetarian meat mash yet.

While she was unwrapping her sandwich, she happened to glance out the window and see the Mintzes' gray minivan backing out of their garage. Bunny was in the passenger seat, riding high like royalty and gazing straight ahead.

Well, fine, then. Be that way. If their father cared so much about his precious rules, he ought to stick around to enforce them.

"I don't remember that *I* wasn't allowed to ride alone

with a boy," Kate had told him when he announced this particular rule.

"I don't remember that any boy asked you," her father had said.

Kate allowed herself a little fantasy: one day Bunny would get old, and she would age in that unfortunate way that blondes so often did. Her hair would become strawlike, and her face would be wrinkly as an apple and ruddier than her lips. She had turned out to be such a disappointment, their father would confide to Kate.

A CONCRETE BENCH stood at the rear of the backyard, mottled and pitted and greenish. Nobody ever sat on it, but today, instead of eating in the kitchen, Kate decided to take her sandwich out there. She settled at one end of the bench with her sandwich plate beside her, and she tipped her head back to stare up into the tree above her. A robin was going crazy on one of the lower branches, hopping about and showering her with agitated *chink-chink* sounds. Maybe it had a nest up there, although she couldn't see one. And in the giant oak across the alley, two other birds, invisible, seemed to be having a conversation. "Dewey? Dewey? Dewey?" one was saying, and the other said, "Hugh! Hugh! Hugh!" Kate couldn't tell whether the second bird was greeting the first one or setting him straight.

After she'd finished gardening she would assemble her mash ingredients in the Crock-Pot, and then she would change all the beds and start a sheet wash.

And after that, what?

She didn't have any friends anymore. They had all moved on in their lives—graduated from college, found jobs in distant cities and even married, some of them. At Christmas they might come back to Baltimore for a visit, but they had stopped phoning her, for the most part. What would they find to talk about? The only time she got a text nowadays was when Bunny was being kept after school and needed a ride home.

Dewey and Hugh had gone quiet now, and the robin had flown away. Kate pretended to herself that the robin had decided she could be trusted. She took a bite of her sandwich and gazed studiously at a nearby cluster of hyacinths to demonstrate that she had no interest in robbing his stupid nest. The tiers of curly white blooms reminded her of the white paper frills on lamb chops.

"Khello?"

She stopped chewing.

Pyotr was coming out the back door; he was descending the back steps. He wore his lab coat today, and it flapped open over his T-shirt as he walked toward her across the grass.

She couldn't believe it. She could not believe that he would have the nerve.

"How'd you get into the house?" she demanded as soon as he was close enough.

"Front door was standing wide," he said.

Damn Bunny to hell.

He stopped when he reached her and stood looking

down at her. At least he had the good grace not to attempt any chitchat.

She couldn't invent a reason for his being there. Surely he must see that she wanted nothing to do with him, even if for some reason her father hadn't yet told him so. And her father *had* told him, she sensed. The other times she'd seen Pyotr, he had arrived in front of her with (it struck her in retrospect) a little bounce, a "Here-I-am!" air, but today he was solemn, chastened, and he held himself with an almost military erectness.

"What do you want?" she asked him.

"I came to offer apology."

"Oh."

"I fear Dr. Battista and I have offended you."

She felt both gratified and humiliated to know that he comprehended this.

"Was inconsiderate of us to ask you to deceive your government," he said. "I think Americans feel guilt about such things."

"It wasn't just inconsiderate," she said. "It was piggish and self-centered and insulting and . . . despicable."

"Aha! A shrew."

"Where?" she asked, and she spun around to look toward the shrubbery behind her.

He laughed. "Very comical," he told her.

"What?"

She turned back to find him smiling down at her, rocking from heel to toe with his hands in his pockets. Apparently he imagined that they were on good terms now. She picked up her sandwich and took a large, defiant bite and started chewing. He just went on smiling at her. He seemed to have all the time in the world.

"You realize you could be arrested," she told him once she'd swallowed. "It's a criminal offense to marry somebody for a green card."

He didn't look very concerned.

"But I accept your apology," she said. "So. See you around."

Not that she had any intention of seeing him ever again.

He let out a long breath and took his hands from his pockets and stepped over to sit beside her on the bench. This was unexpected. Her plate sat between them and she feared for its safety, but if she picked it up he might feel encouraged to move closer. She let it be.

"Was a foolish notion anyhow," he said, speaking to the lawn in general. "It is evident you could choose any husband you want. You are very independent girl."

"Woman."

"You are very independent woman and you have the hair that avoids beauty parlors and you resemble dancer."

"Let's not go overboard," Kate said.

"Resemble flamingo dancer," he said.

"Oh," she said. "Flamenco."

Stomping the floorboards. Made sense.

"Okay, Pyotr," she said. "Thanks for stopping by."

"You are only person I know who pronounces my name right," he said sadly.

She took another bite from her sandwich and chewed it, staring straight out across the lawn now the same way he was doing. But she couldn't help feeling a little stab of sympathy.

"And Dr. Battista!" he said, turning to her suddenly. "Why your name for Dr. Battista is 'Father' but your sister calls him 'Papa'?"

"'Father' is what he told us to call him," she said. "But you know our Bunnikins."

"Ah," he said.

"While we're on the subject," she said, "why do you call him 'Dr. Battista' when he calls you 'Pyotr'?"

"I could never call him 'Louis,'" Pyotr said in a shocked tone. ("Loov-wiss," he made it sound like.) "He is too illustrious."

"He is?"

"In my country he is. I had for many years been hearing about him. When I announced that I am leaving to assist him, there became a great outcry in my institute."

"Is that a fact," Kate said.

"You did not know his reputation? Ha! Is like a proverb we have: 'Man who is respected in rest of the world is not—'"

"Right; I get your gist," Kate said hastily.

"Is true he is sometimes oligarch, but I have observed other men so important act much worse. He does not ever shout! And see how he tolerates your sister."

"My sister?"

"She is empty-head, yes? You know this."

"Airhead," Kate said. "No kidding."

She felt filled with a certain airiness herself, all at once. She started smiling.

"She is puffing her hair and blinking her eyes and abandoning animal proteins. And he does not point it out to her. This is very nice of him."

"I don't think he's being nice," Kate said. "I think he's being predictable. You see it all the time: those mad-genius scientists who go gaga over dumb blondes, the ditzier the better. It's practically a cliché. And naturally the blondes are crazy about *them*; a lot of women are. You should get a load of my father at my aunt Thelma's Christmas parties! All these women flocking around him because they think he's so unreadable and unreachable and mysterious. They think that they're the ones who might finally crack his code."

There was a certain liberation in talking to a man who didn't have a full grasp of English. She could tell him anything and half of it would fly right past him, especially if the words came tumbling out fast enough. "I don't know how Bunny got this way," she told him. "When she was born I more or less thought she was my own; I was at that age when kids like tending babies. And she looked up to me so when she was a little girl; she tried to act like me and talk like me, and I was the only one who could comfort her when she was crying. But after she reached her teens she kind of, I don't know, left me behind. She changed into this whole other person, this *social* person, I don't know; this social, outgoing person.

And somehow she turned *me* into this viperish, disapproving old maid when I'm barely twenty-nine. I don't know how that happened!"

Pyotr said, "Not *all* scientists."

"What?"

"Not *all* scientists prefer blondes," he said, and he flicked a glance at her suddenly from under those half-mast lids. Clearly he hadn't registered a thing she'd said. It made her feel as if she'd gotten away with something.

"Hey," she said. "Would you like the other half of my sandwich?"

"Thank you," Pyotr said. He picked it up unhesitatingly and took a bite. A kind of knot stood out at the angle of his jaw when he chewed. "I think I will call you 'Katya,'" he said with his mouth full.

Kate didn't want to be called "Katya," but since she never had to see him again she didn't bother telling him so. "Oh, well, whatever," she said carelessly.

He asked her, "Why Americans always begin inch by inch with what they say?"

"Pardon?"

"They must begin every sentence with 'Oh . . .' or 'Well . . .' or 'Um . . .' or 'Anyhow . . .' They start off with 'So . . .' when there has been no cause mentioned before it that would lead to any conclusion, and 'I mean . . .' when they have said nothing previous whose significance must be clarified. Right off from a silence they say that! 'I mean . . .' they begin. Why they do this?"

Kate said, "Oh, well, um . . . ," drawing it out long

and slow. For a second he didn't get it, but then he gave a short bark of laughter. She had never heard him laugh before. It made her smile in spite of herself.

"For that matter," she said, "why do *you* begin so abruptly? You just barge into your sentences straight out! '*This* and such,' you begin. '*That* and such,' blunt as a sledgehammer. So definite, so declarative. Everything you say sounds like a . . . governmental edict."

"I see," Pyotr said. Then, as if correcting himself, he said, "Oh, I see."

Now she laughed too, a little. She took another bite of her sandwich, and he took a bite of his. After a minute she said, "Sometimes I think foreigners *like* sounding different. You know? Listen to a foreigner sing an American pop song, for instance, or tell a story where they have to put on a Southern drawl or a cowboy twang. They can do it perfectly, without a trace of an accent! They can mimic us exactly. That's when you see that they don't really want to talk like us at all. They're proud they have an accent."

"I am not proud," Pyotr said. "I would like to not have accent."

He was looking down at his sandwich as he said this— just holding it in both hands and gazing downward, with those lids of his veiling his eyes so she couldn't tell what he was thinking. It occurred to her suddenly that he *was* thinking—that only his exterior self was flubbing his *th* sounds and not taking long enough between consonants, while inwardly he was formulating thoughts every bit as complicated and layered as her own.

Well, okay, a glaringly obvious fact. But still, somehow, a surprise. She felt a kind of rearrangement taking place in her mind—a little adjustment of vision.

She set the crust of her sandwich on her plate and wiped her hands on her jeans. "What will you do now?" she asked him.

He looked up. "Do?" he said.

"About your visa."

"I don't know," he said.

"I'm sorry I can't help."

"It is no problem," he told her. "I say this sincerely. Is kind of you to offer consolation, but I am feeling that things will work out."

She didn't see how they could, but she decided to practice restraint and refrain from telling him so.

He finished his own sandwich, crust and all, and dusted off his palms. He made no move to leave, though. "You have very pretty yard," he said, looking around.

"Thanks."

"You like to garden?"

"Yup."

"Me too," he said.

She said, "I was even thinking I'd be, oh, a botanist or something, before I dropped out of college."

"Why you dropped out of college?"

But she had had enough by now. She saw he must sense she might be softening toward him; he was pressing his advantage. Abruptly, she stood up and said, "I'll just see you to your car."

He stood up too, looking surprised. "There is no need," he told her.

But she started toward the front yard as if she hadn't heard him, and after a moment he followed.

As they rounded the side of the house, the Mintzes' minivan pulled into their driveway and Bunny fluttered a hand out the passenger-side window. She didn't seem the least bit abashed that Kate had caught her riding with Edward. "Hey again, Pyoder," she called.

Pyotr lifted an arm in her direction without responding, and Kate turned and headed back to her gardening. It really was a beautiful day, she realized. She was still mad as hell at her father, but she took some faint comfort in telling herself that at least the man he'd tried to palm off on her was not a complete heel.

CHAPTER SIX

"KATHERINE, MY DEAREST!" HER FATHER SAID. "Darling Kate! Apple of my eye!"

Kate looked up from her book. She said, "Huh?"

"I feel as if a great, huge weight has been lifted off my shoulders," he said. "Let's celebrate. Where's Bunny? Do we still have that bottle of wine around?"

"Bunny's gone to a sleepover," Kate said. She turned a page corner down and laid her book on the couch beside her. "What are we celebrating?"

"Ha! As if you didn't know. Come on out to the kitchen with me."

Kate stood up. She was beginning to feel uneasy.

"That Pyoder is a cagey one, isn't he?" her father asked as he led the way to the kitchen. "He just slipped away from the lab while Bunny and her tutor were there; never said a word. I had no idea he'd gone to see you until he told me the news."

"What news?"

Her father didn't answer; he was opening the refrigerator and stooping to rummage at the back of it.

"What news are you talking about?" Kate asked him.

"Aha!" he said. He straightened and turned toward

her, holding up a Chianti bottle that had been loosely re-corked.

"That's several months old, Father."

"Yes, but it's been in the refrigerator all this time. You know my system. Get me some glasses."

Kate reached up to the top shelf of the china cabinet. "Just tell me what we're drinking to," she said as she handed him two dusty wineglasses.

"Why, Pyoder says you like him now."

"He does?"

"He says you two sat together in the backyard, and you fed him a delicious lunch, and you and he had a nice talk."

"Well, I suppose that all more or less did happen, in a manner of speaking," Kate said. "And? So?"

"So he has hope! He thinks this will work out!"

"Is *that* what he thinks! Oh, hang the man! He's a lunatic!"

"Now, now," her father said genially. He was pouring wine into the glasses, bunching up his mustache as he stood back to assess the level. "Five ounces," he said, mostly to himself. He passed her a glass. "Sixteen seconds, please."

She shut the glass in the microwave and stabbed the appropriate buttons. "What this proves," she said, "is that it doesn't pay to be polite to people. Honestly! He comes to the house uninvited, barges in without my say-so, and it's true the front door was open which is so typical of Bunny, might I add—we could have been robbed blind for all *she* cared—but even so it was boorish of him to take advantage of it. Interrupts my nice quiet lunch, eats half of my roast beef sandwich, which I admit I did offer to him, but still, he could have turned it down; only a foreigner would pounce on it that way—"

"Aren't you going to get that?" her father asked. He meant the microwave, which had dinged some time ago. He indicated it with a tilt of his chin.

"—and then look at how he twists things!" Kate said, exchanging the first glass for the second. She punched the buttons again. "What was I supposed to do: sit there in total silence? Naturally I talked to him, in a minimal kind of way. So now he has the nerve to say I like him!"

"But he *is* likable, isn't he?" her father asked.

"We're not talking about just liking, though," she said. "You're asking me to marry the guy."

"No, no, no! Not immediately," her father said. "Let's not get ahead of ourselves. All I'm asking is that you take some time before you jump into any decision. Give my plan a little thought. Not too *much* thought, of course; it's already April. But—"

"Father," Kate began sternly.

"The wine?" he prompted her, with another tilt of his head.

She retrieved the second glass from the microwave, and he held the first glass aloft. "A toast!" he proposed. "To—"

She felt sure he was going to say "you and Pyoder," but instead he said "keeping an open mind."

He took a sip. Kate did not. She set her glass on the counter.

"Delicious," he said. "I should share my system with *Wine Enthusiast Magazine.*"

He took another, deeper swallow. Now that the weather was warmer, he had abandoned the waffle-knit long-sleeved undershirts he wore all winter. His coverall sleeves were rolled up to expose his bare forearms, which were thin and black-haired and oddly frail. Kate felt an unexpected jolt of pity for him, over and above her exasperation. He was so inept-looking, so completely ill-equipped for the world around him.

Almost gently, she said, "Father. Face it. I will never agree to marry someone I'm not in love with."

"In other cultures," he said, "arranged marriages are—"

"We are not in another culture, and this is not an arranged marriage. This is human trafficking."

"What?"

He looked horrified.

"Well, isn't it? You're trying to trade me off against my will. You're sending me to live with a stranger, *sleep* with a stranger, just for your own personal gain. What is that if not trafficking?"

"Oh, my heavens!" he said. "Katherine. My goodness. I would never expect you to *sleep* with him."

"You wouldn't?"

"No wonder you've been reluctant!"

"Then what *did* you expect?" she asked.

"Why, I just thought . . . I mean, goodness! There's no need for *that* kind of thing," he said. He took another slug of wine. He cleared his throat. "All I had in mind was, we would go on more or less as before except that Pyoder would move in with us. That much, I suppose, is unavoidable. But he would have Mrs. Larkin's old room, and you would stay on in *your* room. I just assumed you knew that. Goodness gracious!"

"It didn't occur to you that Immigration might find that suspicious?" Kate asked him.

"Why would they? Lots of couples have separate bedrooms; Immigration's surely aware of that. We can say Pyoder snores. Maybe he does snore, for all we know. See, now . . ." He started rummaging through his coverall pockets. He brought out his cell phone. "See, I've been reading up," he said. "I know what they look for. We need to document a gradual courtship, to prove to them that . . ." He squinted down at his phone, pressed a button and then another, and squinted again. "Photographs," he told her, handing her the phone. "Taken over time. Recording your shared history."

The screen showed Kate and Pyotr sitting cattycorner from each other at the table in her father's laboratory, Kate on a high stool and Pyotr in a folding chair. Kate wore her buckskin jacket; Pyotr was in his lab coat. They were looking toward the viewer with startled, confused expressions.

She flipped to the next photo. Same pose, except that now Kate was speaking directly to the photographer, revealing two sharp tendons in her neck that she had never noticed before.

The next photo showed her from behind, blurry and distant, pausing on a sidewalk. She had turned halfway toward the man who was following her, but from the rear, it wasn't clear who he was.

In the next, the man had hold of her arm and they were bypassing another couple.

It appeared that her father had been stalking her.

Then she and Pyotr were sitting across from each other at the Battistas' dining-room table, but Bunny was in the foreground and the honey jar she held up partly obscured Pyotr's profile.

And then Pyotr sat on Kate's side of the table and a sliver of Kate stood next to him, minus her head. That was the last photograph.

"I'm going to send you these, as soon as I figure out how," her father said. "I was thinking you should start texting him, too."

"Pardon?"

"I read in the paper the other day that Immigration sometimes asks couples for their cell phones. They go through all their texts to make sure they're really involved with each other."

Kate held the phone toward her father, but he was busy refilling his wineglass. Somehow he'd already emptied it, and now he was emptying the bottle as well. He passed her the glass and said, "Fourteen seconds."

"Only fourteen?"

"Well, it's had time to get warmer now."

He accepted his phone and pocketed it and then stood waiting, while Kate turned away and set his glass in the microwave.

"See, I haven't wanted to talk about this yet," he said,

"but I believe I'm on the cusp of something. I may be nearing a breakthrough, at just the very moment when the powers that be are starting to lose faith in my project. And if Pyoder could stay on at the lab, if we really can accomplish this . . . Do you know what that would mean to me? It's been such a long haul, Kate. A long, weary, *discouraging* haul, let me tell you, and I know sometimes it must have seemed as if it's all I've cared about; I know your mother used to think so—"

He broke off to tilt his chin at the microwave again. Kate took out the glass of wine and handed it to him. This time he drained half the glass in a gulp, and she wondered if that were wise. He was not accustomed to alcohol. On the other hand, maybe it was thanks to the alcohol that he was suddenly so communicative. "My mother?" she prompted him.

"Your mother thought we should have weekends. Vacations, even! She didn't understand. I know *you* understand; you're more like me. More sensible, more practical. But your mother: she was very . . . unsturdy, I would say. She disliked being alone; can you imagine? And the most trivial little thing would send her into despair. More than once, she told me she didn't see any point to life."

Kate clamped her arms across her chest.

"I told her, 'Well, of course you don't, dearest. I can't in good conscience say that there *is* any point. Did you ever believe there was?' This didn't seem to comfort her, though."

"Really," Kate said.

She reached for her wineglass and took a large swig.

"A lot of women, when they have babies they feel happy and fulfilled," she said once she had swallowed. "They don't all of a sudden decide that life is not worth living."

"Hmm?" Her father was staring moodily into the dregs of his own glass. Then he looked up. "Oh," he said, "it was nothing to do with *you*, Kate. Is that what you're thinking? She was feeling low long before *you* were born. I'm afraid it might have been my fault, in part. I'm afraid our marriage may have had a deleterious effect on her. Everything I said, it seemed, she took the wrong way. She thought I was belittling her, behaving as if I were smarter than she was. Which was nonsense, of course. I mean, no doubt I *was* smarter, but intelligence is not the only factor to consider in a marriage. In any event, she couldn't seem to rise above her low spirits. I felt I was standing on the edge of a swamp watching her go under. She did try various different types of therapy, but she always ended up deciding it wasn't helping. And pills, she tried those. All sorts of antidepressants—SSRIs and so forth. None of them worked, and some of them had side effects. Finally a colleague of mine, a fellow from England, told me about a drug he'd invented that they'd begun using in Europe. It hadn't yet been approved in the States, he said, but he had seen it work miracles, and he sent me some and your mother tried it. Well, she became a whole new person. Vibrant! Animated! Energetic! You were in eighth grade by then and she suddenly took an interest, started attending PTA meetings, volunteered to accompany your class on field trips. I had my old Thea back, the woman she'd been when I met her. Then she said she wanted another baby. She had always wanted six children, she said, and I said, 'Well, it's your decision, dear. You know I leave such matters up to you.' Right away she got pregnant, and she went to her doctor to confirm it, and that's when we found out that the miracle drug had damaged her heart. They'd already begun to suspect that in Europe, and they were taking the drug off the market; we just hadn't heard yet."

"*That's* what caused her heart trouble?"

"Yes, and I accept full responsibility for it. If not for me, she would never have known about that drug. Or needed it either, your aunt always claims." He drained off the last of his wine and set his glass a bit too firmly on the counter beside him. "Although," he said after a moment, "I suppose it did provide valuable data for my colleague."

"She went on field trips with me?" Kate asked. She was trying to wrap her mind around this. "She was interested in me? She liked me?"

"Why, of course. She loved you."

"I missed her one good spell!" Kate said. It was almost a wail. "I don't remember it!"

"You've forgotten how you used to go shopping together?"

"We went shopping together?"

"She was so happy, she said, to have a daughter she could do girl things with. She took you shopping for clothes and lunch, and once you went for manicures."

This made her feel eerily disconnected. Not only had she mislaid the memory of experiences she thought she would have treasured all her life, but also, they were experiences that she assumed she would have hated. She couldn't abide shopping! Yet apparently she had gone along willingly, and maybe even enjoyed herself. It was as if Kate the child had been a completely different entity from Kate the grown-up. She looked down at her blunt, colorless nails and could not make herself believe that once they had been professionally filed and buffed and painted with polish.

"So that's why we have our Bunny," her father was saying. There was a blurriness in his voice, perhaps due to the wine, and the lenses of his glasses were misting. "And of course I'm delighted we do have her. She's so pretty to look at and so lighthearted, the way your mother used to be before we married. But she's not, let's say, very . . . cerebral. And she doesn't have your backbone, your fiber. Kate, I know I depend on you too much." He reached out to set his fingertips on her wrist. "I know I expect more of you than I should. You look after your sister, you run the house . . . I worry you'll never find a husband."

"Gee, thanks," Kate said, and she jerked her wrist away from him.

"No, what I mean is . . . Oh, I always put things so awkwardly, don't I. I just meant you're not out where you could *meet* a husband. You're shut away at home, you're puttering in the garden, you're tending children in a pre-school, which, come to think of it, is probably the last place on earth to . . . I've been selfish. I should have made you go back to school."

"I don't want to go back to school," Kate said. She really didn't; she felt a flutter of dismay.

"There are other schools, though, if that was not the right one for you. It's not as if I'm unaware of that. You could finish up at Johns Hopkins! But I've been indulging myself. I told myself, 'Oh, she's young; there's plenty of time; and meanwhile, I get to have her here at home. I get to enjoy her company.'"

"You enjoy my company?"

"It may be, too, that that was another reason I thought of pairing you off with Pyoder. 'I'd still get to keep her around!' I must have been thinking. 'No harm done: it's a marriage only on paper, and she would still be here in the house.' You have every right to be cross with me, Kate. I owe you an apology."

"Oh, well," Kate said. "I guess I can see your side of it."

She was remembering the evening she had come home from college. She had arrived unannounced with several suitcases—all she had taken away with her—and when the taxi dropped her off at the house she'd found her father in the kitchen, wearing an apron over his coveralls. "What are *you* doing here?" he had asked, and she had said, "I've been expelled"—putting it even more baldly than need be, just to get the worst of it over with. "Why?" he had asked, and she had told him about her professor's half-assed photosynthesis lecture. When her father said, "Well, you were right," she had felt the most overwhelming sense of relief. No, more than relief: it was joy. Pure joy. She honestly thought it might have been the happiest moment in her life.

Her father was holding the wine bottle up to the

window now, plainly hoping to find another drop or two in the bottom.

She said, "When you say 'On paper . . .'"

He glanced over at her.

"If it's just a formality," she said, "if it's just some little legal thing that would allow you to change his visa status and after that we could reverse it . . ."

He set the bottle back down on the counter. He stood tensed, possibly not breathing.

"I suppose that's not *that* big a deal," she said.

"Are you saying yes?"

"Oh, Father. *I* don't know," she said wearily.

"But you might consider it. Is that what you're saying?"

"I suppose," she said.

"You really might do this for me?"

She hesitated, and then she gave him a tentative nod. In the very next instant she wondered what on earth she could be thinking, but already her father was pulling her into a fierce, clumsy hug, and then thrusting her away again to gaze exultantly into her face. "You'll do it!" he said. "You really will! You care enough about me to do this! Oh, Kate, my darling, I can't even put into words how grateful I am."

"I mean, it's not as if it would make all that much difference in how I live," she said.

"It will make no difference at all, I swear it. You'll hardly know he's in the picture; everything will go on exactly the same as before. Oh, I'm going to do all I can to arrange it so things will be easy for you. This changes everything! Everything's looking up; somehow I feel certain now that my project's going to succeed. Thank you, sweetheart!"

After a moment, she said, "You're welcome."

"So . . ." he said. "And . . . Kate?"

"What."

"Do you think you could finish my taxes for me? I did try, but"—and here he stood back to spread his spindly arms comically, helplessly—"you know how I am."

"Yes, Father," she said. "I know."

CHAPTER SEVEN

Sunday 11:05 AM

> *Hi Kate I text you!*
> *Hi.*
> *U r home now?*
> *Spell things out, for heaven's sake. You're not some teenager.*
> *You are home now?*
> *No.*

THE BALLERINA DOLL AND THE SAILOR DOLL WERE getting married. The sailor doll wore his same old uniform but the ballerina doll had a brand-new dress of white Kleenex, one sheet for the front and another for the back, held together at the waist with a ponytail scrunchy and billowing out at the bottom because of the tutu underneath it. Emma G. had made the dress, but it was Jilly who'd donated the scrunchy and Emma K. who knew the rules about walking down the aisle and meeting the groom at the altar. Apparently Emma K. had been a flower girl at some point in the recent past. She held forth at length on the concept of the ring-bearer, the bouquet-tossing, and the "skyscraper wedding cake" while the other girls listened, spellbound. It didn't seem to occur to them to consult Kate about these details, although word of her upcoming wedding was what had set all this in motion.

Kate had thought at first that she just wouldn't tell anyone. She would get married on a Saturday—the first Saturday in May, less than three weeks from now—and come in to school the following Monday, nobody any the wiser. But her father was disappointed when he learned that she wasn't spreading the word yet. Immigration was bound to inquire at her place of employment, he said, and it would look mighty suspicious if her coworkers thought she was single. "You should go ahead and announce it," he said. "You should walk in tomorrow all smiles, flash a ring about, make up some good story about your long, slow courtship, so that Immigration will hear every detail if they start asking around."

Immigration was the family's new bugaboo. Kate envisioned Immigration as a "he"—one man, wearing a suit and tie, handsome in the neutral, textureless style of a detective in an old black-and-white movie. He might even have that black-and-white-movie voice, projected-sounding and masterful. "Katherine Battista? Immigration. Like to ask you a few questions."

So she arrived at school the next morning, a Tuesday, wearing her great-aunt's diamond ring, and before she had even checked into Room 4 she went to the faculty lounge, where most of the teachers and a few assistants were standing around the tea kettle, and she silently held her left hand out.

Mrs. Bower was the first to notice. "Oh!" she squawked. "Kate! What is this? Is this an *engagement* ring?"

Kate nodded. She couldn't quite manage the "all smiles" part, because Mrs. Bower taught Room 2—the room where Adam assisted. She was certain to go straight back to Room 2 and tell Adam that Kate was engaged.

Kate had been thinking about the telling-Adam part ever since she had gotten herself into this.

Then all the other women clustered around her, exclaiming and asking questions, and if Kate's behavior seemed subdued they probably chalked it up to her usual unsociableness. "Aren't you the sly one!" Mrs. Fairweather said. "We didn't even know you had a boyfriend!"

"Yeah, well," Kate mumbled.

"Who is he? What is his name? What does he do for a living?"

"His name is Pyoder Cherbakov," Kate said. Without planning to, she pronounced it the way her father pronounced it, making it sound less foreign. "He's a microbiologist."

"Really! A microbiologist! Where did you two meet?"

"He works in my father's lab," she said. Then she glanced toward Mrs. Chauncey and said, "Gosh, nobody's watching the Fours," trying to find an excuse to escape before they could ask more questions.

But of course they didn't let her off that easily. Where was Pyotr from? (He must not be a *Baltimore* boy.) Did her father approve of the match? When would the wedding take place? "So soon!" they said when they learned the date.

"Well, he's been in the picture three years," Kate said. Which was true, strictly speaking.

"But you'll have so much planning to do!"

"Not really; it's going to be very low-key. Just immediate family."

This disappointed them, she could tell. They had imagined attending. "When Georgina got married," Mrs. Fairweather reminded her, "she invited her whole class, remember?"

"This won't be that kind of wedding. We are neither one of us much for dressing up," she said—the unaccustomed "we" sounding as odd to her ears as if she had just popped a stone in her mouth. "My uncle who's a pastor is going to marry us in a private ceremony. Just my father and my sister as witnesses—I'm not even letting my aunt come. She's having conniptions about it."

That it was taking place in a church at all was a compromise. Kate had wanted a quickie affair down at City Hall, while her father had wanted a full-dress ceremony that would photograph well for Immigration. And clearly her coworkers agreed with him; they exchanged sad looks. "The children sat in the pew just behind Georgina's closest relatives, and each of them carried a yellow rose, do you remember that?" Mrs. Fairweather asked Mrs. Link.

"Yes, because Georgina's gown was yellow, the prettiest, palest yellow, and her husband wore a yellow tie," Mrs. Link said. "Both of the mothers were scandalized that she wasn't wearing white. 'What will people think?' they said. 'Whoever heard of a bride not wearing white?'"

"And Georgina said, 'Well, I'm sorry, but I've always looked washed out in white,'" Mrs. Chauncey said.

Sometimes, Kate was downright astonished by how much the women in the faculty lounge sounded like the little girls nattering away in Room 4.

It was Mrs. Chauncey who announced the wedding to Kate's class. "Children! Children!" she said, clapping her plump hands together as soon as they'd finished the "Good Morning" song. "I have wonderful news. Guess who's getting married!"

There was a silence. Then Liam M. ventured, "You, maybe?"

Mrs. Chauncey looked distressed. (She had been married thirty-five years.) "Miss Kate, that's who!" she said. "Miss Kate has gotten engaged. Show them your ring, Miss Kate."

Kate held out her hand. A number of the little girls made murmuring sounds of admiration, but most of the children seemed confused. "Is that okay?" Jason asked her.

"Is what okay?"

"I mean, will your mother let you?"

"Uh . . . sure," Kate said.

And the Samson twins were clearly unhappy. They didn't say anything in class, but out on the playground later that morning they came up to her and Raymond asked, "*Now* who will we marry?"

"Oh, you'll find somebody," she assured them. "Somebody closer to your own age, I bet."

"Who?" Raymond asked.

"Well . . ."

"There's Jameesha," David reminded him.

"Oh, yes."

"And there's—"

"That's okay, I'll take Jameesha."

"But how about me?" David asked him. "Jameesha's always mad at me about something."

Kate didn't get to hear the end of this discussion, because just then Adam came over. He was carrying a tiny pink hoodie and he looked very somber, or perhaps she was only imagining that. "So," he said, arriving next to her. He looked off toward the swings. "I heard the news."

"News?" she asked. (Inanely.)

"They say you're getting married."

"Oh," she said. "That."

"I didn't even know you were seeing anybody."

"I wasn't," Kate said. "I mean, I *kind* of was, but . . . this was very sudden."

He nodded, still looking somber. His eyelashes were so dark and thick that they gave his eyes a sooty effect.

They spent some time watching a three-year-old who had laid herself belly-down on a swing that she'd wound up. She spun around and around, hanging on for dear life, her expression intensely concentrated, and then she got off and tottered away unsteadily, like a very small drunk.

Adam said, "Is that . . . wise, do you think, jumping into such a decision?"

Kate sent him a quick glance, but he was still gazing after the three-year-old and it was impossible to read his expression. "Maybe not," she said. "Maybe it isn't. *I* don't know."

Then after a long pause she said, "This could be, you know, just temporary, though."

Now he did look at her. "Temporary!" he said.

"I mean, who can ever tell if a marriage will last, right?"

The sooty eyes grew darker and narrower. "But it's a *covenant*," he said.

"Yes, but . . . yes, right. A covenant. You're right."

And she was back to feeling too tall again, too out-spoken, too brassy. She took a sudden interest in Antwan, who'd climbed dangerously high on the jungle gym, and she walked off abruptly to deal with him.

Tuesday 2:46 PM

> *Hi Kate! You would like me to walk you from school?*
> *No.*
> *Why not?*
> *It's my day for Extended Daycare.*
> *I walk you later?*
> *No.*
> *You are not polite enough.*
> *Bye.*

A NEW PHOTO: Kate standing stiffly on the front walk, Pyotr standing next to her wearing a wide smile even though he was looking a little pink around the nostrils. His so-called cold was an allergy to something outdoors, it was beginning to seem.

Then Kate and Pyotr sitting on a restaurant banquette. Pyotr's right arm was stretched proprietorially along the back of the seat behind Kate, which gave him a contorted, trying-too-hard aspect because the seat back was fairly high. Also he was frowning slightly with the effort to see in the dimness; he complained that American restaurants were not lit brightly enough. Kate's father had been there too, of course, because someone had to take the photo. He and Kate had each ordered a burger. Pyotr had ordered veal cheeks on a bed of puréed celeriac drizzled with pomegranate molasses, after which he and Dr. Battista fell into a discussion of the "genetic algorithms" of recipes. When Pyotr was listening closely to someone his face took on a kind of peacefulness, Kate noticed. His forehead smoothed, and he grew completely still as he concentrated on the other person.

Next, Kate and Pyotr on the living-room couch, a foot of empty space between them, Pyotr grinning broadly and doing his arm-along-the-seat-back thing while Kate, stony-faced, poked her left hand toward the photographer to display her diamond ring. Or it could have been cubic zirconia; nobody was quite sure. The great-aunt had clerked in a dime store.

Kate and Pyotr doing the dishes. Pyotr, wearing an apron, waved a pre-rinsed plate in the air. Kate stood looking sideways at him as if she wondered who this person was. Bunny, only partly visible, seemed to be wondering who *both* of them were; she rolled her big blue eyes disbelievingly toward the camera.

It was Bunny who showed their father how to forward the photos to Kate's and Pyotr's cell phones, since he himself hadn't the remotest idea. She rolled her eyes again, but she helped him. She made no secret, though, of her horror at the marriage plan. "What are you?" she asked Kate. "Chattel?"

"It's only for a while," Kate told her. "You don't know how desperate things are getting at the lab."

"No, and I don't care. That lab has nothing to do with you."

"It does have to do with Father, though. It's the center of his life!"

"*We* are supposed to be the center of his life," Bunny said. "What is it with him? The man forgets for months at a stretch that we even exist, but at the same time he thinks he has the right to tell us who we can ride in cars with and who we should marry."

"Whom," Kate said automatically.

"Wake up and smell the coffee, sis. He's making a human sacrifice of you, don't you get it?"

"Oh, now, it's not *that* bad," Kate said. "This will only be on paper, remember."

But Bunny was so upset that her Taylor Swift ringtone played nearly all the way through before she could think to answer her phone.

Friday 4:16 PM

> *Hi Kate! I come with you to the grocery store*
> *tomorrow.*
> *I like shopping alone.*
> *I come because your father and I are cooking*
> *supper.*
> *What!*
> *I will pick you up in my car at eight in morning.*
> *Bye.*

HIS CAR WAS an original Volkswagen Beetle; she hadn't seen one of those in years. It was peacock blue, and so weatherworn that it looked not painted but chalked. Otherwise, though, it seemed to be in excellent condition. This struck her as miraculous, in view of the way he treated it. Was there some natural law that decreed that scientists couldn't drive? Or maybe they *could* drive, but they were too immersed in their own esoteric thoughts to bother looking at the road. Pyotr kept looking at Kate instead, turning his face fully toward her to talk while the Beetle careened down 41st Street and the other drivers braked and honked and a tumult of books and lab coats and empty water bottles and fast-food wrappers slid around the backseat. "We get a pork loin," he was saying. "We get cornmeal."

"Watch what you're doing, for God's sake."

"This store will sell maple syrup?"

"Maple syrup! What on earth are you cooking?"

"Braised pork on a bed of polenta drizzled with maple syrup."

"Good God."

"Your father and I have discussed."

"The genetic algorithms of recipes," Kate said, remembering.

"Ah. You were paying attention. You were heeding what I said."

"I was not heeding what you said," Kate told him. "I just couldn't avoid overhearing you blab away in my ear."

"You were heeding me. You like me! You are crazy about me, I think."

"Pyotr," Kate said, "let's get something straight."

"Awk! That was too-big truck for this road."

"I am only doing this to help my father out. He seems to think it's important that you should stay in this country. After you get your green card, you and I will go our separate ways. Not a step of this plan involves anybody being crazy about anybody."

"Or maybe you will decide *not* to separate," Pyotr said.

"What? What are you talking about? Have you heard a word I've been saying?"

"Yes, yes," he said hastily. "I am listening. Nobody shall be crazy about anybody. And now we will go buy pork."

He pulled into the supermarket parking lot and cut the engine.

"Why are we having pork?" Kate asked as she followed him across the lot. "You know Bunny's not going to eat it."

"I am not much concerned about Bunny," he said.

"You're not?"

"In my country they have proverb: 'Beware against the sweet person, for sugar has no nutrition.'"

This was intriguing. Kate said, "Well, in my country they say that you can catch more flies with honey than with vinegar."

"Yes, they *would*," Pyotr said mysteriously. He had been walking a couple of steps ahead of Kate, but now he dropped back and, without any warning, slung an arm around her shoulders and pulled her close to his side. "But why you would want to catch flies, hah? Answer me that, vinegar girl."

"Let go of me," Kate said. Up close, he smelled like fresh hay, and his arm felt steely and insistent. She broke free of him. "Good grief," she said. And the rest of the way across the parking lot, it was she who kept a few steps ahead.

At the entrance to the store she snagged a cart and started inside, but Pyotr caught up with her to reach for the cart and take over. She was beginning to suspect that he had some kind of he-man complex. "What-*ever*," she told him. He merely smiled and cruised along beside her with the empty cart.

For someone who talked so much about vitamins, he was remarkably uninterested in the vegetable section. He languidly tossed in a head of cabbage and then asked, gazing around him, "The cornmeal: where we would find that?"

"You really seem to go for those la-di-da kinds of

dishes," Kate said as she led the way. "Like that thing you ordered in the restaurant, with puréed celeriac."

"I just echoed final item."

"Excuse me?"

"The waiter, when he came to our table: he talked so complicated. He said, 'Like to tell you guys about a few specials this evening . . .'" Pyotr had the waiter's Baltimore accent down pat; it was uncanny. "Then he said things very long and combined; he said the free-range and the stone-ground and the house-cured until I am vertiginous. So I just repeated what came last. 'The veal cheeks on a bed of puréed celeriac,' I repeated, because it was still in my ears."

"Then maybe this evening we could go back to plain old mash," Kate said.

But Pyotr said, "No, I think not." And that was the end of that.

The computer-generated grocery list wasn't much use today. For one thing, they still had a hefty supply of mash left over from last Saturday's batch, which was why Kate had been hoping that she could serve it tonight. This past week had been so different from their usual week, as far as meals were concerned. Not only had her father arranged for that photo-op restaurant dinner with Pyotr, but then the next night Pyotr had insisted on taking *them* to a restaurant (all except Bunny, who had said that enough was enough), and on Tuesday, claiming the need to celebrate a brief, freakish spring snowfall, he had shown up unannounced with a tub of KFC chicken.

And this coming week, at some point, Kate would

have to think up some kind of dinner for Aunt Thelma. Dr. Battista had been making noises about inviting her in to meet Pyotr, along with her husband and perhaps Uncle Theron too, if it didn't conflict with his church obligations. They might as well grit their teeth and get it over with, Dr. Battista said. He and Aunt Thelma were not on the best of terms (Aunt Thelma blamed him for her sister's depression), but "Immigration-wise," he said, "I feel it would be smart to expose as many relatives as possible to your marriage plans. And since you're not letting your aunt attend the wedding, this seems a strategic alternative."

The reason Kate wasn't letting her aunt attend the wedding was that she knew her too well. It would be just like her to show up with six bridesmaids and a full choir.

What to feed her, though? Certainly not meatless mash, although it would have been a convenient way to get rid of those damn leftovers. Maybe just plain chicken; Kate could manage that much, surely. She picked out a couple of roasters while Pyotr was browsing the pork selections, and then she doubled back to the vegetable department for asparagus and russet potatoes.

As she was returning to the meat department, she caught sight of Pyotr from a distance, deep in conversation with a black man in an apron. Pyotr's stretched-out gray jersey and his vulnerable-looking bare neck struck her all at once as oddly touching. It wasn't entirely his fault, she supposed, that he found himself in this peculiar position. And for a moment she tried to imagine how she herself would feel if she were alone in a foreign country, her visa about to expire, no clear notion of where she would go once it did expire or how she would support herself. Plus the language problem! She had been a middling-good language student, once upon a time, but she would have felt desolate if she'd had to actually *live* in another language. Yet here Pyotr stood, blithely engaged in a discussion of pork cuts and displaying his usual elfin good spirits. She had to smile, a little.

When she arrived next to him, though, he said, "Oh! Is my fiancée. This nice gentleman says maybe not loin but fresh ham," and right away she felt annoyed again. "Fiancée": ick. And she had always hated the mealy-mouthed sound of "gentleman."

"Get what you want," she told him. "It's all the same to me." Then she dumped her groceries into the cart and wandered off again.

Pyotr wasn't entirely satisfied with the notion of serving Aunt Thelma roast chicken, it turned out. When Kate made the mistake of telling him her menu plan, after he had caught up with her in the syrup-and-molasses aisle, his first question was "The chickens can be cut into pieces?"

"Why would you want to do that?"

"I am thinking you could make fried, like KFC. You know how to make fried chicken?"

"No."

He waited, looking hopeful.

"But you could learn?" he asked finally.

"I could if I wanted to, I guess."

"And you would want to, maybe?"

"Well, Pyotr, if you like KFC so much, why don't I just buy some?" Kate said. She would love to see the expression on Aunt Thelma's face if she did.

"No, you should be cooking something," Pyotr said. "Something with much labor. You are trying to make your aunt feel welcome."

Kate said, "Once you meet Aunt Thelma, you'll realize that the last thing we want to do is make her feel too welcome."

"But she is *family*!" Pyotr said. He pronounced the word as if it were holy; he surrounded it with invisible cushions. "I want to know all of your family—your aunt and her husband and her son and also your uncle the pastor. I anticipate your uncle the pastor! He will try to convert me, maybe?"

"Are you kidding? Uncle Theron couldn't convert a kitten."

"Theron," Pyotr repeated. He made it sound like "Seron." "You are doing this to torture me?"

"Doing what?"

"So many *th* names!"

"Oh," Kate said. "Yes, and my mother's name was Thea."

He groaned. "What is the surname of these people?" he asked.

After the briefest pause, she said, "Thwaite."

"My God!" He clapped a hand to his forehead.

She laughed. "I'm pulling your leg," she told him. He lowered his hand and looked at her. "I was just kidding," she clarified. "Really their surname is Dell."

"Ah," he said. "You were joking. You made a joke. You were teasing me!" And he started capering around the cart. "Oh, Kate; oh, my comical Kate; oh, Katya mine . . ."

"Stop it!" she said. People were staring at them. "Quit that and tell me which syrup you want."

He stopped capering and selected a bottle, seemingly at random, and dropped it into the cart. "That's kind of small," she said, peering down at it. "Are you sure it'll be enough?"

"We do not want an excess of mapleness," Pyotr said severely. "We want balance. We want subtlety. Oh! If it is very successful, we could serve a maple-syrup dish to your aunt! We could serve chicken on a bed of . . . some unusual substance, drizzled with maple syrup. Your aunt will say, 'What a heavenly dish you are giving me!'"

"That would be a very, very unlikely thing for Aunt Thelma to say," Kate told him.

"I may call her 'Aunt Selma' too?"

"If you mean Aunt *Thelma*, I suggest you wait until she says you can. Anyhow, I don't know why you'd want to claim her as your aunt if you didn't have to."

"But I have never had an aunt!" Pyotr said. "This will be my very first aunt."

"Lucky you."

"I will wait till she gives permission, though, I promise. I will be deeply respectful."

"Don't overdo it on my account," Kate said.

❧

THEN PYOTR HAD to go and tell her father that they had had a "lovely time" grocery-shopping. This was later that afternoon, when the two men were cooking dinner in the kitchen. Kate stepped in from the backyard with her bucket of gardening tools, and her father beamed at her as if she'd just won a Nobel Prize. "You had a lovely time at the grocery store!" he said.

"I did?"

"I *told* you Pyoder was a good fellow! I knew you'd figure it out, eventually! He says you had a lovely, friendly grocery trip together."

Kate sent Pyotr an evil glare. He was smiling modestly with his eyes lowered as he patted spices all over his fresh ham.

"Maybe after supper you two would like to go to a movie," her father suggested.

Kate said, "I'm washing my hair after supper."

"After supper? You're washing your hair after supper? Why are you doing it *then*?"

Kate sighed and slung her bucket into the broom closet.

Pyotr said, "We are wondering if you can be explaining to us what braising is."

"I have no idea what braising is," Kate said. She went to the sink to wash her hands. There were bloody meat wrappers in the sink and a cabbage core, along with several outer leaves. Since her father was fanatic about the clean-as-you-go principle, she knew all too well whom to blame. "Don't you dare leave the kitchen like this when you're finished," she told Pyotr as she dried her hands.

"I will take care of everything!" Pyotr said. "Eddie is staying to dinner?"

"Who's Eddie?"

"Your sister's boyfriend. In the living room."

"Edward, you mean. No, he's not. 'Eddie'! Good grief!"

"Americans love to be called nicknames," Pyotr said.

"No, they don't."

"Yes, they do."

"No, they don't."

"Please!" Kate's father said. "Enough." He was stirring a pot on the stove. He looked toward them with a pained expression.

"Plus, he's not her boyfriend," Kate told Pyotr.

"Yes, he is."

"No, he's not. He's too old to be her boyfriend. He's her tutor."

"Your sister is studying microorganisms?"

"What?"

"Book on her lap is *Journal of Microbiological Methods*."

"It is?"

"Is that a fact!" Dr. Battista marveled. "I didn't even know she was interested!"

"Oh, geez," Kate muttered. She flung her towel onto the counter and turned to leave the kitchen.

"Is like a proverb I know," Pyotr was telling her father as she walked out.

"Spare us," Kate tossed back. In her sneakers, she made no sound as she crossed the hall. She popped through the living-room doorway and said, "Bunny—"

"Eek!" Bunny said, and she and Edward sprang apart.

The Journal of Microbiological Methods was not on her lap anymore. It lay at the far end of the couch. Even so, Kate crossed the room in four strides and picked it up and stuck it in front of Bunny's face. "This is *not* what you need to be learning," she told Bunny.

"Excuse me?"

"We're paying him to teach you Spanish."

"You're not paying him a thing!"

"Well . . . and that's exactly what I meant when I told Father we *should* be paying."

Bunny and Edward looked bewildered.

"Bunny is fifteen years old," Kate told Edward. "She's not allowed to date yet."

"Right," he said. He was less practiced than Bunny at faking self-righteous innocence. He flushed and looked glumly down at his knees.

"She can only see boys in groups."

"Right."

Bunny said, "But he's my—"

"And don't tell me he's your tutor, because why did I have to sign your D-plus Spanish test yesterday?"

"It's the subjunctive?" Bunny said. "I just never have gotten the hang of the subjunctive?" She seemed to be asking whether there was any chance this explanation might be convincing.

Kate turned on her heel and walked out. Before she was halfway across the hall, though, Bunny had jumped up from the couch and come after her. "Are you saying we can't see each other anymore?" she asked. "He's just visiting me at my house! We're not going out on dates or anything."

"The guy must be twenty years old," Kate told her. "You don't find anything wrong with that?"

"So? I'm fifteen years old. A very *mature* fifteen."

"Don't make me laugh," Kate told her.

"You're just jealous," Bunny said. She was following Kate through the dining room now. "Just because you have to settle for Pyoder—"

"His name is Pyotr," Kate said through her teeth. "You might as well learn to pronounce it right."

"Well, la-di-da to you, Miss Frilling-Your-*r*s. At least *I* didn't have to rely on my father to find me a boyfriend."

By the time she was saying this, they had reached the kitchen. The two men glanced over at them, surprised. "Your daughter is a jerk," Bunny told their father.

"I beg your pardon?"

"She is a snoopy, jealous, meddlesome jerk, and I refuse to—and *now* look!"

Her attention had been snagged by something outside the window. The rest of them turned to see Edward slinking past with his shoulders hunched, veering beneath the redbud tree to cross to his own house.

"I hope you're satisfied," Bunny told Kate.

"Why is it," Dr. Battista asked Pyotr, "that whenever I'm around women for any length of time, I end up asking, 'What just happened here?'"

"That is extremely sexist of you," Pyotr said sternly.

"Don't blame *me*," Dr. Battista said. "I base the observation purely on empirical evidence."

Monday 1:13 PM

>*Hi Kate! We went to get marriage license!*
>*Who's we?*
>*Your Father and I.*
>*Well I hope you'll be very happy together.*

CHAPTER EIGHT

"HOW DO YOU DO, PYODER?" AUNT THELMA ASKED.

"Um!" Kate broke in.

Too late, though. "I have been having very bad allergy, but now am feeling better," Pyotr said. "It was maybe the smelly wooden material they put on the ground around bushes."

"Mulch, we call that," Aunt Thelma informed him. "M-U-L-C-H. It's meant to hold the moisture in during our long hot summers. But I very much doubt that that could be what you're allergic to."

It always made Aunt Thelma happy when she could set somebody straight. And Pyotr was smiling into her face so widely and so steadily, clearly preconditioned to adore her—just the sort of thing she found appealing. Maybe the evening would go better than Kate had imagined.

They were assembled in the entrance hall: Kate and her father and Pyotr, and Aunt Thelma and her husband, Uncle Barclay. Aunt Thelma was a tiny, pretty woman in her early sixties, with a smooth blond bob and very bright makeup. She wore a beige silk pantsuit and a filmy, color-splashed scarf wound several times around her neck and flung back over her shoulders. (Kate used to fantasize that her aunt's perennial scarves were meant to hide something—a past surgery or, who knows, maybe a couple of fang marks.) Uncle Barclay was lean and handsome and gray-haired, wearing an expensive-looking gray suit. He headed a high-powered investment firm and seemed to find Dr. Battista and his daughters humorously quaint, like something in a small-town natural history museum. Now he watched them with an indulgent smile, slouching gracefully in the doorway with his hands in his trouser pockets, which caused an elegant drape in the hem of his suit coat.

The rest of them had dressed up to the extent of their abilities. Kate wore her denim skirt with one of her plaid shirts. Pyotr was in jeans—foreign jeans, belted exactly at his waist and ballooning around his legs—but he had added a crisply ironed white shirt and his shoes were not his usual running shoes but snub-nosed brown Oxfords. Even Dr. Battista had made an effort. He had put on his one suit, which was black, and a white shirt and a spindly black tie. He always looked so thin and uncertain when he was out of his beloved coveralls.

"This is very exciting," Aunt Thelma began, at the same time that Kate said, "Let's go to the living room." She and Aunt Thelma frequently experienced an overlapping-speech problem. "Uncle Theron's already here," Kate said as she led the way.

"*Is* he," Aunt Thelma said. "Well, he must have shown up too early, then, because Barclay and I are exactly on time."

Since Uncle Theron had indeed arrived early, by special arrangement so that they could discuss the ceremony, Kate had nothing to say to this.

Aunt Thelma sailed ahead of the rest of them and entered the living room with both arms outstretched, ready to engulf Bunny, who was just rising from the couch. "Bunny, dear!" Aunt Thelma said. "Gracious! Aren't you chilly?"

It was the first really hot day of the year, and Bunny couldn't possibly be chilly. Aunt Thelma was merely pointing out the skimpiness of her sundress, which was the length of a normal person's shirt and tied at the shoulders with huge, perky bows that resembled angel wings. Also, her sandals had no backs to them. A no-no.

One of Aunt Thelma's many instructions to the girls over the years had been: Never wear backless shoes for a social occasion. It was second only to Rule Number One: Never, ever, under any circumstances apply lipstick while at the table. All of Aunt Thelma's rules were etched permanently in Kate's mind, although by natural preference Kate owned no backless shoes anyhow and she never wore lipstick.

Bunny, though, tended not to catch Aunt Thelma's subtexts. She just said, "No, I'm sweltering!" and gave her a peck on the cheek. "Hi, Uncle Barclay," she said, and she gave him a peck too.

"Theron," Aunt Thelma said regally, as if granting a dispensation. Uncle Theron had risen from his chair and was standing with his chubby, blond-furred hands clasped in front of his crotch. He and Aunt Thelma were twins, which explained their alliterative names if not their baby sister's, but Aunt Thelma had "come out first," as she always put it, and she had the firstborn's self-assured edge to her while Theron was a timid man who had never married or, it seemed, had any serious experiences in life. Or maybe he'd just failed to realize if he *had* had them. He always seemed to be blinking at something, as if he were trying to get his mind around the most ordinary human behavior, and in the nonministerial, short-sleeved yellow shirt that he was wearing tonight he had a peeled, defenseless look.

"Aren't you excited?" Aunt Thelma asked him.

"Excited," he repeated in a worried way.

"We're marrying off our Kate! You *are* a dark horse, aren't you?" she said to Kate as she settled herself in an armchair. Pyotr, meanwhile, dragged the rocker he had been sitting on closer to Aunt Thelma. He still had his eyes trained expectantly on her face; he was still beaming. "We didn't even know you had a beau," Aunt Thelma told Kate. "We were afraid Bunny might beat you to the altar."

"Bunny?" Dr. Battista said. "Bunny's fifteen years old." The corners of his mouth were turned down, and he still hadn't taken a seat. He was standing in front of the fireplace.

"Sit, Father," Kate said. "Aunt Thelma, what can I get you to drink? Uncle Theron's having ginger ale."

She mentioned the ginger ale because she had just learned that her father had picked up only one bottle of wine—her mistake, entrusting him with the errand—

and she was hoping no one would ask for any wine until dinner. But her aunt said, "White wine, please," and then turned to Pyotr, who was still waiting with bated breath for any pearls that might drop from her lips. "Tell us, now," she said, "how—?"

"We only have red," Kate said.

"Red it will have to be, then. Pyoder, how—?"

"Uncle Barclay?" Kate said.

"Yes, I'll have some red."

"*How* did you and Kate meet?" Aunt Thelma finally managed to ask.

Pyotr said promptly, "She came to Dr. Battista's lab. I expected nothing. I thought, 'Living at home, no boyfriend . . .' Then she appeared. Tall. Hair like Italian movie star."

Kate left the room.

When she returned with the wine, Pyotr had moved on to her inner qualities and Aunt Thelma was smiling and nodding and looking charmed. "She is somewhat like the girls at home," he was saying. "Honest. Tells what she is thinking."

"*I'll* say," Aunt Thelma murmured.

"But in truth she is kindhearted. Thoughtful."

"Why, Kate!" Aunt Thelma said in a congratulatory tone.

"Takes care of people," Pyotr went on. "Tends small children."

"Ah. And will you continue with that?" Aunt Thelma asked Kate as she accepted her wine.

Kate said, "What?"

"Will you continue at the preschool once you're married?"

"Oh," Kate said. She had thought Aunt Thelma was asking how long she could keep up her charade. "Yes, of course."

"She does not need to," Pyotr said. "I can support her," and he flung out one arm in a grand gesture, nearly knocking over his glass. (He too had opted for wine, unfortunately.) "If she likes, she may retire now. Or go to college! Go to Hopkins! I will pay. She is my responsibility now."

"What?" Kate said. "I'm not your responsibility! I'm my own responsibility."

Aunt Thelma tut-tutted. Pyotr just smiled around the room at the others, as if inviting them to share his amusement.

"Good girl," Uncle Barclay said unexpectedly.

"Well, once you have children that will be a moot point anyhow," Aunt Thelma said. "May I ask what wine we're drinking, Louis?"

"Eh?" Dr. Battista was giving her a distressed look.

"This wine is delicious."

"Oh," he said.

He didn't seem all that thrilled to hear it, even though it might have been the first compliment Aunt Thelma had ever paid him.

"Tell me, Pyoder," Aunt Thelma said, "will any of your family be coming to the wedding?"

"No," Pyotr said, still beaming at her.

"Old classmates, then? Colleagues? Friends?"

"I do have friend from my institute, but he is in California," Pyotr said.

"Oh! Are you close?" Aunt Thelma asked.

"He is in California."

"I mean . . . is he someone you'd want at your wedding?"

"No, no, that would be ridiculous. Wedding is five minutes."

"Oh, surely it will last longer than *that*."

Uncle Theron said, "Take his word for it, Thelma; they've asked for the stripped-down version."

"My kind of ceremony," Uncle Barclay said approvingly. "Short and sweet."

"Hush, Barclay," Aunt Thelma told him. "You don't mean that. This is a once-in-a-lifetime event! That's why I can't believe that you and I are not invited."

There was an uncomfortable silence. Finally Aunt Thelma's own social instincts got the better of her; she was the one who spoke up. "Tell us, Kate, what will you wear?" she asked. "I would love to take you shopping."

"Oh, I think I'm set," Kate said.

"I know you couldn't have hoped to fit into the dress your poor mother wore to *her* wedding . . ."

Kate wished that, just once, Aunt Thelma would refer to her mother without using the word "poor."

Maybe her father felt the same way, because he interrupted to ask, "Isn't it time to get supper on the table?"

"Yes, Father," Kate said.

As she stood up, Uncle Theron was asking Pyotr whether he was allowed to practice religion in his country. "Why I would want to do that?" Pyotr said, looking honestly curious.

Kate felt glad to be leaving the room.

The men had done the cooking earlier that afternoon—sautéed chicken on a bed of grated jicama, drizzled with pink-peppercorn sauce since the other evening's maple syrup had not been deemed a success. All Kate had to do was set the platter out on the table and toss the salad. As she walked back and forth between the kitchen and the dining room, she caught snatches of the talk in the living room. She heard Uncle Theron utter the phrase "premarital counseling," and she stiffened, but then Pyotr said, "Is so confusing, the two types of 'counsel.' I am mixed up how to spell them," and Aunt Thelma was delighted to jump in and give him an English lesson, so the moment passed. Kate wasn't sure whether he'd changed the subject on purpose.

He could surprise her sometimes, she had found. It had emerged that it was dangerous to assume that he wouldn't catch her nuances; he caught a lot more than he let on. Also, his accent was improving. Or was it just that she had stopped hearing it? And he had started beginning his sentences with a "well" or an "oh," on occasion. He seemed to take great delight in discovering new idioms— "jumped the gun," for instance, which had sprinkled his conversations for the past several days. ("I was thinking the evening news would be on, but I see that I . . ." and then a weighty pause before "*jumped the gun!*" he finished up triumphantly.) Now and then, an expression he used would strike her as eerily familiar. "Good grief," he said, and "Geez," and once or twice, "It was semi-okay." At such moments, she felt like someone who had accidentally glimpsed her own reflection in a mirror.

He was still undeniably foreign, though. Even his posture was foreign; he walked in a foreign way that was more upright, shorter in stride. He had the foreigner's tendency toward bald, obvious compliments, dropping them with a thud at her feet like a cat presenting her with a dead mouse. "Even a fool can see you're after something," she would say, and he would affect a perplexed look. Hearing him now in the living room, pontificating about the hidden perils of ice water, she felt embarrassed by him, and embarrassed *for* him, and filled with a mixture of pity and impatience.

But just then a pair of sharp heels came clicking across the dining room. "Kate? Do you need any help?" Aunt Thelma called in a loud, false, carrying voice, and a moment later she slipped through the kitchen door to put an arm around Kate's waist and whisper, on a winey breath, "He's a *cutie*!"

So Kate was being too critical, clearly.

"With that golden cast to his skin, and his eyes tilting up at the corners . . . And I love that ropy yellow hair," her aunt said. "He must have some Tartar in him, don't you think?"

"I have no idea," Kate said.

"Or is it 'Tatar.'"

"I really don't know, Aunt Thelma."

OVER SUPPER, Aunt Thelma proposed that she should take charge of the reception. "What reception?" Kate asked, but her father drilled her with a narrow stare. She could guess his meaning: he was thinking that a reception would look so convincing to Immigration.

"I have to admit that this must be a genuine marriage," the black-and-white detective would report to his superiors, "because the bride's family threw a big shindig for them."

Immigration often used 1940s slang words, in Kate's fantasies.

"It's just selfish not to let your friends and relations be part of your happiness," Aunt Thelma was saying. "Why, what about Richard and his wife?"

Richard was Aunt Thelma and Uncle Barclay's only child, a blow-dried, overconfident type who worked as a lobbyist in Washington and had a habit of drawing himself up and taking a deep, portentous, whiskery-sounding breath through his nose before delivering one of his opinions. He couldn't have cared less about Kate's happiness.

"I suppose it's your decision if you don't want us all at the ceremony," Aunt Thelma told her. "I'm not pleased about it, but this is not about me, I suppose. However, we should be allowed to take part in the occasion *somehow* or other."

It was like blackmail. Kate could imagine Aunt Thelma parading in front of the church with a picket sign if she weren't allowed her precious reception. She looked toward Pyotr, who was still wearing his huge, hopeful smile. She looked toward Uncle Theron—deliberately bypassing her father—and he was nodding at her encouragingly.

"Well," she said finally. "Well, I'll think about it."

"Oh, goody. This is so, so perfect, because I've just redone the living room," Aunt Thelma said. "You'll love what I've covered the couches in: this gorgeous satin-stripe fabric that cost an arm and a leg, but it was worth every penny. And I've opened out the seating arrangement so the room can hold forty people now. Fifty, in a pinch."

"Fifty people!" Kate said. This was exactly why she hadn't wanted her aunt to come to the wedding: she just somehow ran away with things. "I don't even know fifty people," Kate told her.

"Oh, you must. Old school friends, neighbors, fellow teachers . . ."

"Nope."

"How many *do* you know, then?"

Kate thought. "Eight?" she suggested.

"Kate. There are more than eight people at the Little People's School alone."

"I just don't like crowds," Kate told her. "I don't like mingling. I don't like feeling guilty I'm not moving on and talking with somebody new."

"Ah," Aunt Thelma said. A calculating look came over her face. "How about a little-bitty sit-down dinner, then?"

"How big is little-bitty?" Kate asked warily.

"Well, my table only seats fourteen, so you know it can't be *too* big."

Fourteen people sounded to Kate like quite a lot, but it was better than fifty. "Well . . ." she said, and then her father jumped in to say, "Let's see, now: there would be you and Pyoder, me and Bunny, Thelma and Barclay and Theron, and Richard and his wife, and, oh, maybe our neighbors, Sid and Rose Gordon; they were so nice to us after your mother died. And then . . . how about what's-her-name?"

"Who are you talking about?"

"Your best friend from high school, what's-her-name."

"Oh. Alice. She's married now," Kate said.

"Good. She can bring her husband."

"But I haven't seen her in years!"

"Oh, I remember Alice. She was always so polite," Aunt Thelma said. "So, how many does that make?" She started counting on her fingers. "Nine, ten . . ."

"It's not as if we're trying to meet a minimum requirement," Kate told her.

"Eleven, twelve . . ." Aunt Thelma said, pretending Kate hadn't spoken. "Thirteen," she finished. "Oh, dear. Thirteen at the table: unlucky."

"Maybe add Mrs. Larkin," Dr. Battista suggested.

"Mrs. Larkin is dead," Kate reminded him.

"Ah."

"Who's Mrs. Larkin?" Aunt Thelma asked.

"The woman who used to tend the girls," Dr. Battista said.

"Oh, yes. She died?"

"We could have Edward!" Bunny piped up.

"Why would you want to invite your Spanish tutor to a wedding reception?" Kate asked her, evilly.

Bunny slumped lower in her seat.

"Louis," Aunt Thelma said, "is that sister of yours still alive?"

"Yes, but she lives in Massachusetts," Dr. Battista said.

"Or . . . I know you must have one favorite colleague at the Little People's School," Aunt Thelma told Kate. "Some special friend there?"

Kate pictured Adam Barnes sending her a sooty-eyed gaze over Aunt Thelma's Wedgwood china. "None," she said.

There was a silence. They were all looking at her reproachfully—even Uncle Theron, even Pyotr.

"What's wrong with thirteen at the table?" she asked them. "Are you all really that superstitious? I don't want *any* at the table! I don't know why we're doing this! I thought we were just going to have a simple little no-frills ceremony, Father and Bunny and Pyotr and me. Everything's getting out of control here! I don't know how this happened!"

"There, there, dear," Aunt Thelma said. She stretched a hand across the table to pat Kate's place mat, which was the only part of her she could reach. "Thirteen at the table will be fine," she said. "I was just trying to observe the conventions, that's all; we're not the least bit superstitious. Don't you trouble your head about it. It will all be taken care of. Tell her, Pyoder."

Pyotr, who was seated next to Kate, leaned closer to sling an arm around her shoulders. "Do not worry, my Katya," he said, breathing pink-peppercorn fumes.

"*Sweet*," Aunt Thelma cooed.

Kate pulled away and reached for her water glass. "I just don't like fuss," she told them all, and she took a drink of water.

"Of course you don't," Aunt Thelma said soothingly. "And there's not going to *be* any fuss; you'll see. Louis, where's that wine? Pour her a glass of wine."

"We finished it, I'm afraid."

"This is stress, that's all. It's bridal jitters. Now, Kate, I just want to ask you one more teeny, tiny question and then I'll shut up: you're not going away on the same day as your wedding, are you?"

"Going away?" Kate said.

"On your honeymoon."

"No."

She didn't bother explaining that they wouldn't be taking a honeymoon.

"Wonderful," Aunt Thelma said. "I always think it's such a mistake, starting a long demanding trip right on the heels of the ceremony. So this means we can have our little party in the evening. *So* much nicer. We'll make it early, because you'll have had a big day. Five or five-thirty or so, for the drinks. Now. That's all I'm going to say.

We're going to change the subject now. Isn't the chicken *interesting*! And you men did this? I'm impressed. Bunny, are you not having any?"

"I'm a vegetarian?" Bunny said.

"Oh, yes. Richard went through that stage too."

"It's not a—?"

"Thank you, Aunt Thelma," Kate said.

For once, she really meant it. She found it oddly comforting that her aunt was proving so unflappable.

IT WASN'T BRIDAL jitters.

It was "Why is everyone going along with this? Why are you allowing this? Isn't anyone going to stop me?"

The previous Tuesday—Kate's day for Extended Daycare—she had returned to Room 4 after herding the last child into the last parent's car, and all the teachers and all the assistants had jumped up from the miniature chairs shouting, "Surprise! Surprise!" In the short time that she had been gone, they had assembled from wherever they'd been hiding to cover Mrs. Chauncey's desk with a paper tablecloth and set out refreshments and paper cups and a stack of paper plates, and on the Lego table an upside-down lace parasol spilled tissue-wrapped gifts. Adam was strumming his guitar and Mrs. Darling was holding court behind the punch bowl. "Did you know? Did you guess?" they kept asking Kate, and she said, "It never crossed my mind," which was absolutely true. "I don't know what to say!" she kept saying. They pressed their gifts on her with long-winded explanations: these mugs were ordered in blue but when they arrived they were green; this salad bowl was dishwasher-proof; she was welcome to exchange this carving set if she already had one. They settled her in the place of honor—Mrs. Chauncey's desk chair—and served her pink-and-white cupcakes and homemade brownies. Adam sang "Bridge Over Troubled Water," and Mrs. Fairweather asked if they could see a photo of Pyotr. (Kate showed them the restaurant photo on her cell phone. Several people said he was good-looking.) Georgina wanted to know if Kate was planning to bring him to Room 4 for Show and Tell, but Kate said, "Oh, he can't possibly spare the time away from his research"—picturing, meanwhile, how Pyotr would have reveled in being put on display, how he would have turned the whole event into some kind of circus. And Mrs. Bower advised her to make it clear from the get-go that he should pick his own socks up.

It seemed they viewed her differently now. She had status. She mattered. All at once they were interested in what she had to say.

She hadn't fully understood that before this, she *hadn't* mattered, and she felt indignant but also, against all logic, gratified. And also fraudulent. It was confusing.

Would getting married have any effect on her probation? She couldn't help wondering. She hadn't been called to the office even once since she had announced her engagement, she realized.

Adam's gift was a dream catcher. The hoop was made of willow, he said. He had wound it in strips of suede, and then he had added beads like those on the dream catcher he had given Georgina for her coming baby, and feathers like those on the dream catcher he had given Sophia. "Now, this open space at the center," he said, taking it from Kate to demonstrate, "is supposed to let the good dreams slip through, and this webbing around the edge is supposed to block the bad dreams."

"That's lovely, Adam," Kate said.

He placed it in her hands again. He seemed sad about something, or was she deluding herself? He looked directly into her eyes and said, "I want you to know, Kate, that I wish you only good in your life."

"Thank you, Adam," she said. "That means a great deal to me."

The forecast had been for rain that day, and Kate had taken the car to work. Driving home, with mugs and pots and candlesticks rattling in the backseat among her father's lab supplies, she had smacked the steering wheel with the flat of her hand. "'That's lovely, Adam,'" she quoted herself in a high-pitched, mincing voice. "'That means a great deal to me.'"

And she balled up her fist and punched her own forehead.

Aunt Thelma asked Kate if she were planning to be Kate Cherbakov (pronouncing it as her brother-in-law did). "Definitely not," Kate said. Even if this marriage had not been temporary, she was opposed to the notion of brides changing their names. And Pyotr, to her relief, chimed in with "*No*, no, no." But then he added, "Will be Shcherbakov-*ah*. Female ending, because she is girl."

"Woman," Kate said.

"Because she is woman."

"I'm sticking with Battista," Kate told her aunt.

Uncle Theron said, perhaps in context, "I was telling Pyoder in the living room that I like to suggest a little counseling session to couples before I marry them."

"Oh, what a good idea!" Aunt Thelma exclaimed, as if this were the first she'd heard of it.

"We don't need counseling," Kate said.

"Issues like whether you plan to change your last name, though—" Uncle Theron began.

"Do not worry," Pyotr said hastily. "Is not important. Is only a brand of canned peaches."

"Excuse me?"

"We'll settle it between ourselves," Kate told everyone. "Who wants more chicken?"

The chicken was all right, she supposed, but the pink-peppercorn sauce tasted weird. She was looking forward to raiding her stash of beef jerky as soon as she was alone again.

"I don't know whether Kate mentioned it," Aunt Thelma was saying to Pyotr, "but I'm an interior decorator."

"Ah!"

Kate had the impression that Pyotr didn't have the slightest inkling what an interior decorator was.

"Will you two be living in a house, or in an apartment?" Aunt Thelma asked him.

"Apartment, I think you would call it," Pyotr said. "Is inside a house, however. Widow's house; Mrs. Murphy's. I have top floor."

"But after they marry, he's moving in with us," Dr. Battista said.

Aunt Thelma frowned. Pyotr frowned too. Bunny said, "With us?"

"No," Pyotr said, "I have whole top floor of Mrs. Murphy's house, rent-free because I lift Mrs. Murphy from wheelchair to car and I change her light bulbs. Is only a walk to Dr. Battista's lab, and every window I look out of, I see trees. This spring there is a bird nest! Living room, kitchen, two bedrooms, bathroom. No dining room, but kitchen has table."

"It sounds darling," Aunt Thelma said.

"After the wedding, though, he'll live here," Dr. Battista said.

"I am allowed to use whole backyard, big, large, huge, sunny backyard, because Mrs. Murphy cannot go there in wheelchair. I plant cucumbers and radishes. Kate could maybe plant also." He turned to Kate. "You wish to plant vegetables? Or only flowers."

"Oh," she said. "Well, yes, I'd like to plant vegetables. At least, I think I would. I've never had a vegetable garden before."

"But I thought we discussed this," Dr. Battista said.

"We discussed this and I said no," Pyotr said.

Aunt Thelma took on a gleeful expression. "Louis," she said, "face it. Your little girl has grown up."

"I realize that, but the understanding was that she and Pyoder will live here."

Bunny said, "No one told *me* that! I thought they were living at Pyoder's! I thought I was going to get Kate's room now. With the window seat?"

"It makes much more sense for them to live here," her father told her. "We would just rattle around in this big house all by ourselves."

"Whatever happened to 'Whither thou goest, I will go'?" Bunny asked.

Uncle Theron cleared his throat. "Actually," he said, "those words were spoken to a mother-in-law. People never seem to realize that."

"To a *mother*-in-law?"

"Is entire top floor of house," Pyotr was telling Dr. Battista. "Second bedroom is study now, but I am going to change it to bedroom for Kate."

Aunt Thelma sat up alertly. Her husband grinned and said, "Well, now. I seriously doubt if Kate will require her own bedroom."

Aunt Thelma waited for Pyotr's response as intently as a pointer narrowing in on a quail, but Pyotr was too busy staring down Dr. Battista.

It could be like the coed dorm Kate had lived in while she was in college, she thought. She had loved the coed dorm. She had felt very free there, very casual and natural, and the boys there had been not dates but comfortable acquaintances.

She wondered if Pyotr liked chess. He and she could play chess in the evenings, maybe.

"I blame that old popular song," Uncle Theron was saying. "'Whither thou goest . . .'" he started singing in a fine-grained, slightly quavery tenor.

"Bunny is too young to be at home without supervision," Dr. Battista told Pyotr. "You of all people should be aware of my long hours."

It was true. Bunny would have the house stocked with teenage boys as quick as a wink. Kate experienced a pang of loss as she saw the big, large, huge, sunny backyard slipping out of her grasp.

But Pyotr said, "You can hire a person."

This was also true. Kate perked up.

Aunt Thelma said, "Can't argue with that, Louis. Ha! Seems you've met your match."

"But . . . wait!" Dr. Battista said. "This is not at all how I planned it! You're talking about an entirely different setup here."

Aunt Thelma turned to Kate and said, "It would be my pleasure to come to your apartment and give you two a free consultation. If this is some old Hopkins professor's house, I'll bet it has all kinds of potential."

"Oh, yes, lots," Kate said, because it would look suspicious if she admitted she had never laid eyes on the place.

DESSERT WAS JUST store-bought ice cream, because neither Pyotr nor Dr. Battista had had any other ideas. When they'd looked hopefully at Kate, she had said,

"Well, I'll see what I can find." So at the end of the meal she went out to the kitchen and took a carton of butter pecan from the freezer. As she was setting a row of bowls on the counter, the door to the dining room swung open and Pyotr walked in. He came up next to her and elbowed her in the ribs. "Quit that," she told him.

"Is going well, no?" he murmured in her ear. "I think they like me!"

"If you say so," she said, and she started scooping ice cream.

Then he flung an arm exuberantly around her waist and pulled her close and kissed her cheek. For a moment, she didn't resist; his arm enclosed her so securely, and his fresh-hay smell was quite pleasant. But then, "Whoa!" she said, jerking away. She turned to confront him. "Pyotr," she said sternly. "You remember what we agreed on."

"Yes, yes," he said, and he stood back and held up both palms. "Yes, nobody shall be crazy about anybody," he said. "I can help you carry these bowls in?"

"Please do," she told him, and he picked up the first two she'd filled and backed out the swinging door to the dining room.

It was true that they seemed to like him. She saw that while they were eating their ice cream—Uncle Barclay quizzing him about whether his country had hedge funds, Uncle Theron more interested in whether his country had ice cream, Aunt Thelma leaning toward him in an intimate way to suggest that he call her "Aunt Thelma." (Which he immediately shortened to "Aunt

Thel," or more accurately, "Aunt Sel.") Dr. Battista had been in a silent sulk ever since the housing discussion, but the three guests were acting quite animated.

Well, no wonder. They were happy to be getting rid of her.

She had always been such a handful—a thorny child, a sullen teenager, a failure as a college student. What was to be done with her? But now they had the answer: marry her off. They would never have to give her another moment's thought.

So when Uncle Theron reminded her that she and Pyotr would need to apply for a marriage license, she said pointedly, "Yes, Father and Pyotr already saw to that. And Father has the form he wants me to fill out for Immigration." And she sent a challenging look around the table.

This should have made her aunt and her uncles sit up and take notice, but Uncle Theron just nodded and then they all went back to talking. It was much more convenient to pretend they hadn't understood her.

"Wait!" she wanted to tell them. "Don't you think I'm worth more than this? I shouldn't have to go through with this! I deserve to have a real romance, someone who loves me for myself and thinks I'm a treasure. Someone who showers me with flowers and handwritten poems and dream catchers."

But she kept quiet and stirred her ice cream in her bowl.

CHAPTER NINE

A COUPLE OF DAYS BEFORE THE WEDDING, PYOTR drove over to the house after work so that he and Kate could load her belongings into his car. There weren't all that many: just the clothes from her bureau, packed in a couple of suitcases, and a carton containing her shower gifts, and a garment bag filled with the clothes that had hung in her closet. The suitcases and the carton fit easily into Pyotr's trunk. He laid the garment bag full length across the backseat.

Bunny had greeted Pyotr tepidly and then wandered off somewhere, and Dr. Battista was still at the lab. Kate suspected him of staying away to make a point. He had acted noticeably aloof ever since the decision about her new living arrangements.

Pyotr lived in one of those big old faculty houses within shouting distance of the Johns Hopkins campus, a white clapboard Colonial with faded green shutters. He parked at the front curb, although a driveway lay to one side. He told Kate that he wasn't supposed to block Mrs. Liu's exit; Mrs. Liu was Mrs. Murphy's live-in attendant.

They moved everything into the house in one trip— Kate lugging the suitcases, Pyotr carrying the carton and the garment bag, which he had draped over his shoulder. On the stoop he set down the carton to unlock the front door. "After we carry things up we go to visit Mrs. Murphy," he told her. "She is wanting to meet you."

"Is she okay with my moving in like this?" Kate thought to ask. (Belatedly, it was true.)

"She is okay. Just worries you will say in a while we must move to place of our own."

Kate gave a little snort. No doubt Mrs. Murphy was visualizing some wifey type in a ruffled apron.

The front hall was dim and musty-smelling. A giant gilt-framed mirror loomed over a claw-footed mahogany buffet, and the doors on either side were closed tightly, which was reassuring. Kate wouldn't have to greet the two women every time she went in or out. Also the rest of the house was less dark, she could tell. The stairs in front of her glowed with the late-afternoon sunlight that filtered through a window above them, so that the higher she and Pyotr climbed, the brighter it grew.

The hallway on the next level was carpeted, but the top level—onetime servants' quarters, Kate surmised—had bare pine floorboards and honey-colored wood trim instead of the somber trim of the rest of the house. Kate found it a relief. No door closed this level off, but it was high enough so she couldn't hear any sounds from below. She could tell she would feel private here.

Pyotr led the way to the right, toward a room down the hall. "This will be yours," he told her. He stood back to let her enter and then followed her inside.

It had been serving as his study, clearly. A mammoth desk crowded with computer equipment filled one end of it, and a daybed covered in a garish leopard-print velour stood along the opposite wall. Next to the window was a bureau, antique-looking and small but adequate for Kate's needs, and in the corner sat a dowdy skirted armchair with an ottoman.

"Desk will go to living room," Pyotr told her. He heaved the carton onto the bureau and went to the closet to hang the garment bag. "Later we get a smaller desk, for if you become a student."

Kate said, "Oh! Well. Thank you, Pyotr."

"Mrs. Murphy thinks maybe *she* can give us desk. She has many extra furnitures."

Kate set her suitcases down and went to look out the window. Below her lay the backyard, long and green and framed by shrubbery, some of which she thought might be rosebushes. She had never had enough sun before for roses. At the far end of the yard, just inside the picket fence, she spotted a rectangle of spaded earth that must be Pyotr's vegetable garden.

"Come see the rest of apartment," he told her.

He returned to the doorway but then stood aside to let her go first, and as she walked past him she became acutely aware of his physical proximity. For all her thoughts about how this apartment would be just another coed dorm, it occurred to her that in fact, she was going to be living alone with a man; and when he crossed the hall to open another door and say, "*My* room," she barely glanced in (double bed, nightstand . . .) before backing away. Perhaps he sensed her discomfort, because he quickly shut the door again. "Bathroom," he said, waving toward the half-open door at the end of the hall, but he didn't suggest she step inside. "Is only the one; I am sorry we must share."

"Oh, that's okay; at home I share with *two* people," she said, and she gave a little laugh, but he didn't laugh himself.

He led her next to the living room, which contained only a sagging couch, a fake-woodgrain coffee table, and an old-fashioned tube TV on a wheeled metal cart. "Couch looks old but is soft," he said. He seemed to be studying the couch intently; there was nothing more to be seen in this room, but he made no move to leave.

"One time in high school," he said, "I went home with classmate to work on project. I slept the night there. In my bed I heard his parents talk downstairs. See, this classmate was not orphan boy but normal."

Kate glanced at him curiously.

"I heard just the parents' voices, not words. Parents sat together in the living room. Wife said, 'Mumble mumble?' Husband said, 'Mumble.' Wife said, 'Mumble, mumble, mumble?' Husband said, 'Mumble mumble.'"

Kate couldn't imagine where Pyotr was heading with this.

He said, "You would maybe sit sometimes in this living room with me? You would say 'Mumble?' And I would say 'Mumble mumble.'"

"Or *you* could say 'Mumble?' and *I* could say 'Mumble

mumble,'" Kate suggested. Meaning that she saw no reason why he couldn't be the tentative one and she the more definite. But she could tell he didn't get her point. He looked at her with his forehead crinkling. "Sure," she said finally. "We could do that sometimes."

"O-*kay*!" he said, and he let out an enormous breath and started smiling.

"Kitchen?" she reminded him.

"Kitchen," he said, and he waved her toward the door.

The kitchen lay at the rear of the house, nearest the top of the stairs. It must once have been a storeroom; the walls were cedar, still faintly aromatic. There was a 1950s look to it that was oddly appealing: rusty white metal cabinets, peeling Formica counters, a thickly painted white wooden table with two red chairs. "Nice," Kate said.

"You like it?"

"Yup."

"You like the whole place?"

"Yup."

"I know it is not fancy."

"It's very nice. Very comfortable," she said, and she meant it.

He let out another breath. "Now we go meet Mrs. Murphy," he said.

Standing back again to let her leave the room first, he drew himself inward to allow an exaggerated amount of space for her to pass, as if to make it clear that he would not presume. Evidently she hadn't managed to hide the awkwardness she was feeling.

❧

Mrs. Murphy was a heavyset, gray-haired woman in a lace-trimmed dress and orthopedic shoes. Mrs. Liu was tiny and wiry, and like many older Asian women she wore what could have been men's clothes: an untucked khaki work shirt and boxy brown trousers and blindingly white sneakers. The two of them seemed embedded among the antimacassared chairs and the fussy little tables and the shelves of bric-a-brac, and they emerged only by degrees, Mrs. Liu pushing Mrs. Murphy's wheelchair forward several seconds after Pyotr and Kate stepped through the door. "Is this our Kate?" Mrs. Murphy called out.

Kate almost looked behind her for someone else; it seemed so unlikely that she could be "our" Kate. But Mrs. Murphy was holding out both hands, forcing Kate to step closer and take them in her own. Mrs. Murphy's hands were large and thick-fingered and meaty. She was so large all over, in fact, that Kate wondered how Pyotr could lift her. "You look just the way Pyoder described you," Mrs. Murphy was saying. "We thought maybe he was overstating out of smittenness. Welcome, dear Kate! Welcome to your new home."

"Well . . . thanks," Kate said.

"Has he given you the grand tour yet?"

"I have showed her everywhere except yard," Pyotr said.

"Oh, you have to see the yard, of course. We hear you're going to be planting up a storm."

"Well, um, if that's all right with *you*," Kate said. It

occurred to her that she had no idea if Mrs. Murphy had been consulted.

"It's more than all right," Mrs. Murphy said, at the same time that Mrs. Liu put in, "Will be flowers, though, yes?" Although Mrs. Liu's accent was very different from Pyotr's, she seemed to have the same trouble with pronouns. "This Pyoder is all *useful* things! Cucumbers, cabbages, radishes! She has no poetry."

"*He* has no poetry," Pyotr corrected her. (Not even Pyotr confused his genders.) "Kate will plant flowers and vegetables both. Maybe will someday be botanist."

"Good! You should be botanist too, Pyoder. Get outdoors in sunshine. See how pale?" Mrs. Liu asked Kate. "He is like mushroom!"

If Mrs. Liu were standing closer to Pyotr, she would have nudged him in the ribs, Kate suspected. In fact, both women were looking at him with amusement and affection, and Pyotr was positively basking under their gaze. He wore a serene half-smile and he slid his eyes toward Kate as if to make sure she appreciated his position here.

"But enough about our mushroom man," Mrs. Murphy announced. "Kate, you'll have to tell us what you need for the apartment. Besides a desk, that is; we already know you need a desk. But how about in the kitchen? Did you find enough utensils?"

"Oh, yes," Kate said. She hadn't so much as opened a drawer in the kitchen, but somehow she felt the urge to live up to Mrs. Murphy's notion of her. "Everything looks great," she said.

"You should check our kitchen for duplicates," Mrs.

Murphy told Mrs. Liu. In turning, she let one foot slip off her footrest, and Pyotr bent without her noticing to lift it back into place. "I know we have at least two electric mixers," she was saying. "The stand mixer and the handheld one. Surely we don't need both."

"*Maybe* not . . ." Mrs. Liu said in a doubtful tone.

"We will go see yard now," Pyotr decided. "Talk about mixers some other time."

"All right, Pyoder. Come visit us again, Kate! And you be sure to let us know about any little thing that's lacking."

"Sure," Kate said. "Thanks." And then—evidently still under the spell of Mrs. Murphy's notion of her—she stepped forward and gave Mrs. Murphy both her hands again.

Out on the stoop, Pyotr said, "You liked them?"

"They seemed really nice," Kate said.

"They liked *you*," he said.

"They don't know me!"

"They know you."

He was leading the way around the side of the house now, toward the picket fence that separated the front yard from the rear. "In garage," he said, "are garden tools. I will show you where I hide key."

He lifted the latch of the gate and then stepped back to let her go through. Again he allowed far more space than she needed, but it crossed her mind now that it might be for his sake as much as for hers. Both of them, for some reason, seemed to be feeling a little shy with each other.

CHAPTER TEN

ON HER WEDDING MORNING, KATE OPENED HER eyes to find Bunny sitting at the foot of her bed. "What, are you checking out my window seat?" she asked, although Bunny wasn't even looking at the window seat. She was sitting tailor-fashion in her baby-doll pajamas, staring at Kate intently as if willing her to wake up.

"Listen," she told Kate. "You don't have to do this."

Kate reached behind her to prop her pillow against her headboard. She glanced toward the sky outside; there was a whiteness to the light that made her wonder if rain might be on the way, although the forecast was for sunshine. (Aunt Thelma had been reporting the forecast throughout the past week, because she was hoping to serve drinks on her patio before the "wedding banquet," as she had taken to calling it.)

"I know you think you're just doing a little something on paper to fool Immigration," Bunny said, "but this guy is starting to act like he owns you! He's telling you what last name to use and where to live and whether to go on working. I mean, I do think it would be nice if I could have a bigger room, but if the price for that is my only sister getting totally tamed and tamped down and changed into some whole nother person—"

"Hey. Bun-Buns," Kate said. "I appreciate the thought, but do you not know me even a little? I can handle this. Believe me. It's not as if I haven't dealt my whole life with an . . . oligarch, after all."

"An . . ."

"I'm not that easily squashed. Trust me: I can take him on with one hand tied behind me."

"Okay," Bunny said. "Fine. If your idea of fun is sparring and squabbling, so be it. But you're going to have to be *around* him all the time! Nobody's even mentioned how soon you'll be allowed to divorce him, but I bet it's a year at least and meanwhile you're sharing an apartment with someone who doesn't say please or thank you or smile when you'd expect him to and thinks 'How are you?' means 'How *are* you?' and stands too close to people when he talks and never tells them, 'I think maybe perhaps such-and-such,' but always, flat-out, 'You are wrong,' and 'This is bad,' and 'She is stupid'; no shades of gray, all black and white and 'What I say goes.'"

"Well, part of that is just a matter of language," Kate said. "You can't always be bothered with 'please' and 'maybe' when you're struggling to get your basic message across."

"And the worst of it is," Bunny said, as if Kate hadn't spoken, "the *worst* is, it won't be any different from the fix you're in here—living with a crazed science person who's got a system for every little move you make and spouts off his old-man health theories every chance he gets and measures the polyphenols or whatever in every meal."

"That's not true at all," Kate said. "It will be a *lot* different. Pyotr's not Father! He listens to people, you can tell; he pays attention. And did you hear what he said the other night about how maybe I'd want to go back to school? I mean, who else has ever suggested that? Who else has even given me a thought? Here in this house I'm just part of the furniture, somebody going nowhere, and twenty years from now I'll be the old-maid daughter still keeping house for her father. 'Yes, Father; no, Father; don't forget to take your medicine, Father.' This is my chance to turn my life around, Bunny! Just give it a good shaking up! Can you blame me for wanting to try?"

Bunny looked at her dubiously.

"But thank you," Kate thought to add, and she sat forward and patted Bunny's bare foot. "You're nice to be concerned."

"Well," Bunny said. "Don't say I didn't warn you."

Not until she'd left the room did Kate realize that Bunny hadn't ended a single one of her sentences with a question mark.

IT FELT STRANGE to have their father home in the daytime. He was sitting at the breakfast table when Kate came downstairs, a cup of coffee at his elbow and the newspaper spread before him. "Morning," Kate told him, and he glanced up and adjusted his glasses and said, "Oh. Good morning. Do you know what's going *on* in the world?"

"What?" Kate asked him, but he must have been referring to the news in general because he just waved a hand despairingly toward the paper and then returned to his reading.

He was wearing a pair of his coveralls. This was fine with Kate, but when Bunny walked into the kitchen a moment later she said, "You are *not* going to the church dressed like that."

"Hmm?" her father said. He turned a page of his paper.

"You have to show some respect, Papa! This is some people's house of worship; I don't care what you believe personally. You need to at least put on a regular shirt and trousers."

"It's Saturday," her father said. "Nobody else will be there, just us and your uncle."

"What kind of photo will it make for Immigration, though?" Bunny asked. She could be surprisingly crafty, on occasion. "You in your work outfit. Sort of obvious, don't you think?"

"Ah. Yes, you have a point," he said. He sighed and folded his newspaper and stood up.

Bunny herself was wearing her angel-winged sundress, and Kate—motivated by a vague sense that she owed it to Uncle Theron—had put on a light-blue cotton shift that dated from college. She wasn't accustomed to wearing pale colors and she felt uncomfortably conspicuous; she wondered if she seemed to be trying too hard. Apparently Bunny approved, though. At least, she offered no criticisms.

Kate took a carton of eggs from the fridge and asked Bunny, "Want an omelet?" but Bunny said, "No, I'm going to make myself a smoothie."

"Well, be sure you clean up, then. Last smoothie you made, the kitchen was a disaster."

"I cannot wait," Bunny said, "till you are out of this house and not breathing down my neck all the time."

Evidently she had overcome her concern about palming off her only sister.

A few days ago, Kate had hired a woman named Mrs. Carroll to come in every afternoon and do a little light housekeeping and serve as a companion to Bunny till Dr. Battista got home from work. Mrs. Carroll was the aunt of Aunt Thelma's maid, Tayeema. Aunt Thelma had first suggested Tayeema's younger sister, but Kate wanted someone seasoned who wouldn't be susceptible to whatever Bunny tried to put over on her. "She is a whole lot cagier than some might realize," Kate had told Mrs. Carroll, and Mrs. Carroll had said, "I hear you; yes, indeed."

After breakfast, Kate went back upstairs and packed her last few odds and ends into her canvas tote. Then she changed her sheets for Bunny. She supposed this room would look very different the next time she laid eyes on it. There would be photos and picture postcards bristling around the mirror, and cosmetics crowding the bureau top, and clothes strewn across the floor. The thought didn't disturb her. She had used this room up, she felt. She had used this *life* up. And after Pyotr got his green card she was not going to move back home, whatever her father might fantasize. She would find a place of her own, even if all she could afford was a little rented room somewhere. Maybe she would have her degree by then; maybe she'd have a new job.

She dumped her sheets in her hamper. They were Mrs. Carroll's to deal with now. She picked up her tote and went back downstairs.

Her father was waiting in the living room, sitting on the couch drumming his fingers on his knees. He wore his black suit; once urged, he had gone all out. "Ah, there you are!" he said when she walked in, and then he rose to his feet and said, in a different voice, "My dear."

"What?" she asked, because it seemed he was about to make some sort of announcement.

But he said, "Ah . . ." And then he cleared his throat and said, "You're looking very grown up."

She was puzzled; he had last seen her just minutes ago, looking exactly as she looked now. "I *am* grown up," she told him.

"Yes," he said, "but it's somewhat of a surprise, you see, because I remember when you were born. Neither your mother nor I had ever held a baby before and your aunt had to show us how."

"Oh," Kate said.

"And now here you are in your blue dress."

"Well, shoot, you've seen this old thing a million times," Kate said. "Don't make such a big deal of it."

But she was pleased, in spite of herself. She knew what he was trying to say.

It crossed her mind that if her mother had known too—if she had been able to read the signals—the lives of all four of them might have been much happier.

For the first time, it occurred to her that she herself was getting much better at reading signals.

HER FATHER DROVE, because being a passenger made him nervous. Their car was an elderly Volvo with countless scuff marks on the bumpers from other times he had driven, and the backseat was heaped with the mingled paraphernalia of their three lives—a rubber lab apron, a stack of journals, a construction-paper poster featuring the letter *C*, and Bunny's winter coat. Kate had to sit back there because Bunny had snagged the front seat licketysplit. When the car jerked to an especially sudden stop at a traffic light on York Road, half of the journals slid onto Kate's feet. The expressway would have been smoother, not to mention faster, but her father didn't like merging.

Rhodos 3 for $25, she read as they passed the garden center where she sometimes shopped, and all at once she wished she were shopping there today, having a normal Saturday morning full of humdrum errands. It had turned out sunny, in the end, and you could tell by the slow, dreamy way people were drifting down the sidewalks that the temperature was perfect.

She was feeling as if she couldn't get quite enough air in her lungs.

Uncle Theron's church was called the Cockeysville Consolidated Chapel. It was a gray stone building with a miniature steeple on the roof—a sort of shorthand steeple—and it lay just behind the section of York Road that featured clusters of antique stores and consignment shops. Uncle Theron's black Chevy was the only car in the lot. Dr. Battista pulled up next to it and switched the ignition off and collapsed for a moment with his forehead on the steering wheel, the way he always did when he had managed to get them someplace.

"No sign of Pyoder yet," he said when he finally looked up.

Pyotr was in charge of the morning rounds today at the lab. "See?" Dr. Battista had said earlier. "From now on I'll have a trusted son-in-law whom I can depend on to spell me." However, he had already brought up several details that he worried Pyotr might chance to overlook. Twice before they left the house he had said to Kate, "Should I just telephone him and find out how things are going?" but then he had answered his own question. "No, never mind. I don't want to interrupt him." This may have been due not only to his phone allergy but also to the recent shift in his and Pyotr's relationship. He still hadn't quite gotten over his sulk.

They went to the rear of the building, as Uncle Theron had instructed them, and knocked at a plain wooden door that could have led to somebody's kitchen. Its windowpanes were curtained in blue-and-white gingham. After a moment the gingham was drawn aside and Uncle Theron's round face peered out. Then he smiled and opened the door for them. He was wearing a suit and tie, Kate was touched to see—treating this like a real occasion. "Happy wedding day," he told her.

"Thanks."

"I just got off the phone with your aunt. I imagine she was hoping against hope for a last-minute invitation, but she claimed she was only calling to ask if I thought Pyoder would object to champagne."

"Why would he object to champagne?"

"She figured he might expect vodka."

Kate shrugged. "Not as far as I know," she said.

"Maybe she was thinking he might want to smash his glass in the fireplace or something," Uncle Theron said. He was a good deal more cavalier about his sister when he was not in her presence, Kate noticed. "Come on into my office," he said. "Does Pyoder know that he should knock on the back door?"

Kate sent a glance toward her father. "Yes, I told him," he said.

"We can look at the vows while we're waiting. I know we agreed that you'll do just the bare minimum, but I want to show you what your choices are so you'll know what you'll both be promising."

He led them down a narrow corridor to a small room crammed with books. Books overflowed the shelves and towered in piles on the desk and the seats of the two folding chairs and even the floor. Only the swivel chair behind the desk was usable, but Uncle Theron must have felt that it would have been rude to sit down and let the three of them remain standing. He leaned back against the front of his desk, half sitting on the edge of it, and plucked a book from the top of one stack and opened it to a dog-eared page. "Now, the beginning," he said, running a finger along one line. " 'Dearly beloved' and such. You have no objection to that, I assume."

"No, that's okay."

"And should I ask, 'Who gives this woman?'"

Dr. Battista drew a breath to answer, but Kate jumped in with "No!" so she didn't hear whatever it was that he had planned to say.

"And I'm guessing we'll do without the promise to obey—knowing you, Kate, heh-heh. Well, in fact almost no one keeps the 'obey' in, these days. We'll just proceed straight to 'For better or worse.' Will 'For better or worse' be all right?"

"Oh, sure," Kate said.

It was nice of him to be so accommodating, she thought. He hadn't said a word about the Battistas' known lack of religion.

"You'd be surprised at what some couples want omitted nowadays," he said, closing the book and laying it aside. "And then the vows they write for *themselves*: some of those you wouldn't believe. Such as 'I promise not to talk more than five minutes a day about the cute things the dog did.'"

"You're kidding," Kate said.

"I'm not, I'm afraid."

She wondered if she could get Pyotr to promise to stop quoting proverbs.

"How about photographs?" Dr. Battista asked.

"How about them?" Uncle Theron said.

"May I take some? During the vows?"

"Well, I suppose so," Uncle Theron said. "But these are very *brief* vows."

"That's all right. I'd just like to get, you know, a record. And maybe you could snap a photo of the four of us together, afterward."

"Certainly," Uncle Theron said. He looked at his watch. "Well! All we need now is a groom."

It was 11:20, Kate already knew, because she had just checked her own watch. They had arranged to do this at 11:00. But her father said confidently, "He'll be along."

"Is he bringing the license?"

"I have it." Dr. Battista pulled it from his inner breast pocket and handed it to him. "Then on Monday we'll get things started with Immigration."

"Well, let's go ahead to the chapel where you can all wait more comfortably, shall we?"

"They have to be actually married before they can apply," Dr. Battista said. "It needs to be a *fait accompli*, evidently."

"Have you met Miss Brood?" Uncle Theron asked. He had stopped at another doorway leading off from the corridor. A pale woman in her mid-forties, her short fair hair drawn girlishly back from her forehead with a blue plastic barrette, glanced up from her desk and smiled at them. "Miss Brood is my right hand," he told them. "She's here seven days a week sometimes, and it's only a part-time position. Avis, this is my niece Kate, who's getting married today, and her sister, Bunny, and my brother-in-law, Louis Battista."

"Congratulations," Miss Brood said, rising from her chair. She had turned a bright pink, for some reason. She was one of those people who look teary-eyed when they blush.

"Tell them how you got the name 'Avis,'" Uncle Theron said. Then, without waiting for her to speak, he said to the others, "She was delivered in a rental car."

"Oh, Reverend Dell," Miss Brood said with a tinkly laugh. "They don't want to hear about that!"

"It was an unexpected birth," Uncle Theron explained. "Unexpectedly rapid, that is. Of course the birth itself was expected."

"Well, naturally! It's not as if Mama *intended* to have me in the car," Miss Brood said.

Dr. Battista said, "Thank God it wasn't a Hertz."

Miss Brood gave another tinkly laugh, but she kept her eyes on Uncle Theron. She was fiddling with the strand of white glass beads at her throat.

"Well, moving right along . . ." Uncle Theron said.

Miss Brood went on smiling as she lowered herself to her chair again with a scooping motion at the back of her skirt. Uncle Theron led the rest of them on down the corridor.

The chapel itself, which Kate had seen on several long-ago Christmas Eves and Easter Sundays, was a modern-looking space, with wall-to-wall beige carpeting and plain clear windows and blond wooden pews. "Why don't you all have a seat," Uncle Theron told them, "and I'll head back to my office where I can hear when Pyoder knocks."

Kate had been worrying about that—whether they might miss Pyotr's knock—so she was glad to see him go. Also, they wouldn't have to make small talk if they were on their own. They could sit in silence.

She listened closely to her uncle's footsteps receding down the corridor, because she was wondering if he would pause or at least slow down as he approached Miss Brood's doorway. But no, he hurried right past, oblivious.

"This church is where your mother and I were married," Dr. Battista said.

Kate was startled. She had never thought to ask where they had married.

Bunny said, "Really, Papa? Was it a big fancy wedding with bridesmaids?"

"Oh, yes. Yes, she had her heart set on the whole damn farce," he said. "And Theron had just been hired here as assistant pastor, so nothing would do but that he should officiate. My sister had to come all the way from Massachusetts, bringing my mother. My mother was still alive in those days though not in the best of health, but oh, it was 'We need to have your family at this' and 'Haven't you got any friends? Any colleagues?' My postdoc served as my best man, I seem to recall."

He rose and began pacing up and down the center aisle. He always grew restless when he had to sit idle for any time. Kate looked toward the pulpit, which was made of the same blond wood as the pews. A gigantic book, presumably a Bible, lay open on top of it, with several red ribbon bookmarks hanging out of it, and in front of the pulpit was a low wooden altar with a vase of white tulips centered on a doily. She tried to picture her mother standing there as a bride with a younger, less stuffy version of her father, but all she could summon up was the image of a limp invalid in a long white dress, alongside a bald and stooped Dr. Battista consulting his wristwatch.

A text message came in for Bunny; Kate recognized the tweeting sound. Bunny drew her phone from her purse and looked at it and giggled.

Their father stopped beside a pew and took a leaflet from the hymnal rack. He studied the front of it and the back, and then he returned it to the rack and resumed pacing.

"I hope nothing's gone wrong at the lab," he told Kate the next time he passed her.

"What could go wrong?" she asked him.

She honestly wanted to know, because whatever it was would be preferable to Pyotr's simply deciding he found it too off-putting to marry her no matter how advantageous it was. "Would not be worth it," she could hear him saying. "Such a *difficult* girl! So unmannerly."

But all her father said was "Anything could go wrong. Any number of things. Oh, I had a feeling I shouldn't leave it in Pyoder's hands! I realize the fellow's phenomenally able, but still, he isn't me, after all."

Then he continued toward the rear of the church.

Bunny was typing a text now. *Tap-tap-tap*, as rapid as the telegraph keys in old movies, using both her thumbs and hardly needing to look at the screen.

Eventually, Uncle Theron reappeared. "So . . ." he called from the doorway. He walked toward the pew where Bunny and Kate were sitting, and Dr. Battista reversed course to join them.

"So, does Pyoder have to come from very far away?" Uncle Theron asked.

"Just my lab," Dr. Battista told him.

"Is he subject to a foreign standard of time?"

He was looking at Kate as he asked this. She said, "A foreign . . . ? Well, maybe. I'm not sure."

Then she realized from his expression that she *ought* to be sure, if they had been dating for long. She would have to remember that for their interview with Immigration. "Oh, he's hopeless!" she would say merrily. "I tell him we're due at our friends' house at six and he doesn't even start dressing till seven."

If they ever actually got so far as an interview.

"Perhaps a phone call to find out if he needs directions," Uncle Theron said.

It was silly of her, she knew, but Kate didn't want to make a phone call. She was reminded of those obsessive discussions that girls had in seventh grade—how they wouldn't like to be seen "chasing a boy." Even if this was the boy (so to speak) who was marrying her, it felt wrong. Let him show up as late as he liked! See if *she* cared.

Lamely, she said, "He's probably on the road. I wouldn't want to distract him."

"Just send him a text," Bunny told her.

"Well, um . . ."

Bunny clucked and returned her phone to her purse and then held a hand toward Kate, palm up. Kate stared at it a moment before she understood. Then, as slowly as possible, she dug her own phone from her tote and passed it over.

Tap-tap-tap, Bunny went, without even seeming to think about it. Kate sent a sidelong glance toward what she was writing. "Where r u," she read, beneath the last message Pyotr had sent Kate, which dated from a couple of days ago and said simply, "Okay bye."

This seemed significant now.

No answer. None of those little dots, even, that meant he was working on an answer. They all looked helplessly at Uncle Theron. "Perhaps a phone call?" he suggested again.

Kate steeled herself and took her phone back from Bunny. At the same instant, it made a soft swooping sound, which startled her so that she fumbled and dropped it, but only in her lap, luckily. Bunny gave another cluck and picked it up. "'A terrible event,'" she read out.

Their father said, "What!" He leaned past Uncle Theron and grabbed the phone out of Bunny's hand and stared at it. Then he started typing. Just with one index finger, it was true, but still, Kate was impressed. They all watched him. Finally he said, "*Now* what do I do?"

"What do you mean, what do you do?" Bunny asked him.

"How do I send it?"

Bunny tsked and took the phone from him and punched the screen. Peering over her shoulder, Kate read their father's message: "What what what."

There was a wait. Dr. Battista was breathing oddly.

Then another swooping sound. "'Mice are gone,'" Bunny read out.

Dr. Battista made a strangled, gasping noise. He buckled in the middle and crumpled onto the pew in front of them.

To Kate, the word "mice" made no sense, for a moment. Mice? What did mice have to do with anything? She was waiting for news of her wedding. Uncle Theron seemed equally uncomprehending. He said, "Mice!" with a look of distaste.

"The mice in Father's lab," Bunny explained to him.

"His lab's got mice?"

"It *has* mice."

"Yes . . ." Uncle Theron said, clearly not seeing the distinction.

"Guinea-pig mice," Bunny elaborated.

Now he looked thoroughly confused.

"I can't take it in," Dr. Battista was saying faintly. "I can't seem to absorb this."

Another swooping sound came from the phone. Bunny held it up and read out, "'The animal-rights activists stole them the project is in ruins all is lost there is no hope.'"

Dr. Battista groaned.

"Ah, yes, *that* kind of mice," Uncle Theron said, his forehead clearing.

"Does he mean the PETA people?" Bunny asked everyone. "Is there some rule that grown-ups aren't allowed to abbreviate, or what? 'PETA,' you idiot! Just say 'PETA,' for God's sake! 'Animal-rights activists,' ha! The guy is so . . . plodding! And notice how all at once he puts a 'the' every place he possibly can, even though he almost never says 'the' when he's talking."

"All those years and years of work," Dr. Battista said. He was doubled over now with his head buried in his hands, so that it was hard to make his words out. "Those years and years and years, all down the drain."

"Oh, dear, now surely it can't be *that* bad," Uncle Theron said. "I'm sure this is repairable."

"We'll just buy you some new mice!" Bunny chimed in. She handed the phone back to Kate.

Kate was beginning to grasp the situation finally. She told Bunny, "Even you ought to know that only those mice will do. They're at the end of a long line of generations of mice; they were specially bred."

"So?"

"How did these people get *into* the lab?" Dr. Battista wailed. "How did they know the combination? Oh, God, I'll have to start over from scratch, and I'm too old to start from scratch. It would take me another twenty years at the very least. I'll lose all my funding and I'll have to close the lab and drive a taxi for a living."

"Heaven *forbid*!" Uncle Theron said in real horror, and Bunny said, "You're going to make me drop out of school and get a job, aren't you. You're going to make me go to work serving raw bloody sirloins in some steakhouse."

Kate wondered why they were both contemplating careers they were so unsuited for. She said, "Stop it, you two. We don't know for sure yet whether—"

"Oh, what do *you* care?" her father demanded, raising his head sharply. "You're just glad, I bet, because now you don't have to get married."

Kate said, "I don't?"

Her uncle said, "Why would she *have* to get married?"

"And you!" Dr. Battista told Bunny. "So what if you drop out of school? No great loss! You've never shown the least bit of aptitude."

"Poppy!"

Kate was staring at the hymnal rack in front of her. She was trying to get her bearings. She seemed to be experiencing a kind of letdown.

"So that's it," her father said bleakly. "Excuse me, Theron, will you? I need to get down to my lab." He stood up by inches, like a much older man, and stepped into the aisle. "Why should I even go on living anymore?" he asked Kate.

"I haven't the faintest idea," she snapped.

She would be reclaiming her old room, it appeared. Her life would pick up where it had left off. On Monday when she went in to work she would explain that things just hadn't panned out. She would tell Adam Barnes that she wasn't married after all.

This didn't cheer her up in the least. Adam had nothing to do with her, really. He would always make her feel too big and too gruff and too shocking; she would forever be trying to watch her words when she was with him. He was not the kind of person who liked her true self, for better or worse.

This last phrase sent a little echo of sadness through her. It took her a moment to recollect why.

She rose and followed Bunny into the aisle. It felt as if she had lead in her stomach. All the color seemed to have been washed out of the room, and she saw how bland it was—a dead place.

She and Bunny stood waiting while their father shook their uncle's hand—or more like *clung* to his hand, with both of his own, as if hanging on for dear life. "Thank you anyhow, Theron," he said in a funereal voice. "I apologize for taking up your—"

"Khello?"

Pyotr was standing in the corridor doorway, with Miss Brood smiling anxiously behind his left shoulder. He wore an outfit so shabby that he looked like a homeless person: a stained white T-shirt torn at the neck and translucent with age, very short baggy plaid shorts that Kate worried might be his underwear, and red rubber flip-flops. "You!" he said too loudly. It was Bunny he was addressing. He charged into the chapel, and Miss Brood melted away again. "Do not think for one minute that you will not be arrested," he told Bunny.

She said, "Huh?"

He arrived directly in front of her and set his face too close to hers. "You . . . vegetable eater!" he told her. "You bleedy-heart!"

Bunny took a step backward and dabbed at her cheek with the heel of one hand. He must have been spitting as he talked. "What is *with* you?" she asked him.

"You went to lab in dead of night; I know you did. I

do not know where you took mice but I know it was you who did this thing."

"Me!" Bunny said. "You think it was *me* who did it! You honestly believe I would mess up my own father's project! You're nuts. Tell him, Kate."

Dr. Battista managed to slip in between them at this point. He said, "Pyoder, I need to know. How bad is it?"

Pyotr turned away from Bunny to clap a hand heavily on Dr. Battista's shoulder. "Is bad," he told him. "This is the truth. Is bad as it can get."

"They're *all* gone? Every one?"

"Every one. Both racks empty."

"But how—?"

Pyotr was walking him toward the front of the chapel now, his hand still resting on Dr. Battista's shoulder. "I wake up early," he said. "I think I will go to lab early so I am in time for wedding. I get to door; is locked the same as always. I punch combination. I go inside. I go to mouse room."

They slowed to a stop a few feet from the altar. Uncle Theron and Kate and Bunny stayed where they were, watching. Then Pyotr turned to look back at Kate. "Where *are* you?" he asked her.

"Me?"

"Come on! We get married."

"Oh, well," Dr. Battista said, "I don't know if that's really . . . I think I'd just like to get on down to the lab now, Pyoder, even if there's nothing to—"

But Kate said, "Wait till we say our vows, Father. You can check the lab afterward."

"Kate Battista!" Bunny said. "You are surely not going ahead with this!"

"Well . . ."

"Did you hear how he just talked to me?"

"Well, he's upset," Kate told her.

"I am *not* goddamned *upset*!" Pyotr bellowed.

"You see what I mean," Kate told Bunny.

"Come here *now*!" Pyotr shouted.

Uncle Theron said, "Goodness, he *is* upset," and he chuckled, shaking his head. He walked up the aisle to the altar, where he turned and held both arms out from his sides like an annunciating angel. "Kate, dear?" he asked. "Coming?"

Bunny gave a hiss of disbelief, and Kate turned and handed her tote to her. "Okay, fine," Bunny told her. "Be like that. The two of you deserve each other."

But she accepted the tote, and she trailed after Kate up the aisle.

At the altar, Kate took her place next to Pyotr. "I at first did not understand it," Pyotr was telling Dr. Battista. "Was obvious what had happened, but still I did not understand. I am just staring. Two empty racks and no cages. Painted letters on wall next to racks, painted directly on wall: ANIMALS ARE NOT LAB EQUIPMENT. This is when I think to call police."

"The police: oh, well, what can the police do?" Dr. Battista said. "It's too late now for all that."

"The police take a very, very long time and when they finally come they are not intelligent. They say to me, 'Can you describe these mice, sir?' 'Describe!' I say. 'What to describe? They are ordinary *Mus musculus*; enough is said.'"

"Ah," Dr. Battista said. "Quite right." Then he said, "I don't see why *I* had to get dressed up if you didn't."

"She is marrying me, not my clothes," Pyotr said.

Uncle Theron cleared his throat. He said, "Dearly beloved . . ."

The two men turned to face him.

"We are gathered here in the presence . . ."

"There must be some way they can track them down, though," Dr. Battista murmured to Pyotr. "Hire a rat terrier or something. Don't they keep dogs for such purposes?"

"Dogs!" Pyotr said, turning slightly. "Dogs would eat them! You want this?"

"Or ferrets, perhaps."

"Do you, Katherine," Uncle Theron was saying, in an unusually firm voice, "take this man, Pyoder . . ."

Kate could sense Pyotr's tension from the extreme rigidity of his body, and her father was jittering with agitation on the other side of him, and she could feel the waves of Bunny's disapproval behind her. Only Kate herself was calm. She stood very straight and kept her eyes on her uncle.

By the time they got to "You may kiss the bride," her father was already turning to leave the altar. "Okay, we go now," Pyotr said, even while he was ducking forward to give Kate a peck on the cheek. "The policemen want—" he told Dr. Battista, and then Kate stepped squarely in front of him and took his face between both of her hands and kissed him very gently on the lips. His face was cool but his lips were warm and slightly chapped. He blinked and stepped back. "—policemen want to talk to you too," he said faintly to Dr. Battista.

"Congratulations to both of you," Uncle Theron said.

CHAPTER ELEVEN

IN ORDER TO GET INTO PYOTR'S CAR, KATE HAD TO enter from the driver's side and struggle past the stick shift to the passenger's side. This was because the passenger-side door seemed to have been caved in by something, and it no longer opened. She didn't ask what had happened. It was pretty clear that Pyotr had been driving even more distractedly than usual.

She put her tote on the floor among an assortment of discarded flyers, and then she fumbled beneath her for whatever the lump was that she was sitting on. It turned out to be Pyotr's cell phone. Once he was settled behind the wheel, she held it toward him and asked, "Were you texting while *driving*?" He didn't respond; just grabbed it away from her and stuffed it into the right front pocket of his shorts. Then he twisted the key in the ignition, and the engine roared to life with a grinding sound.

Before he could back out of his parking space, though, Dr. Battista rapped his knuckles on Pyotr's side window. Pyotr cranked the window down and barked, "What!"

"I'm dropping Bunny off at home and then I'm going straight to the lab," Dr. Battista told him. "I'll talk to the police after I check things out. See you two at the reception, I guess."

Pyotr merely nodded and shifted violently into reverse.

Barreling down the Jones Falls Expressway, he seemed to feel the need to relive every last second of the tragedy. "I stand there; I think, 'What am I seeing?' I think, 'I will just blink my eyes and then everything will be normal.' So I blink, but racks are still empty. No cages. Writing on wall looks *shouting*, looks loud. But room is very, very still; has no motion. You know that mice are always moving. They rustle and they squeak; they hurry to the front when they hear anybody coming; they find humans . . . promising. Now, nothing. Stillness. Four, five cedar chips on bare floor."

His window was still open and the wind was whipping her hair into snarls, but Kate decided not to mention it.

"I am so not wanting to believe it that I turn and walk into other room. As if mice just maybe took themselves elsewhere. I say, 'Khello?' I don't know why I say, 'Khello?' Is not as if they could answer."

"You want to veer left at this fork," Kate said, because they were traveling so fast that it seemed he might not be planning to do that. At the last second he swerved violently, throwing her against her door, and shortly afterward he took a speedy right onto North Charles Street without checking for traffic. (*He* certainly felt no hesitation about merging.) "I never trusted that Bunny, right from start," he told Kate. "So baby-acting. Is like what they say in my country about—"

"Bunny didn't do this," Kate told him. "She doesn't have the nerve."

"Of course she did it. I told police she did it."

"You what?"

"Detective wrote her name down in notebook."

"Oh, Pyotr!"

"She knows combination of lock, and she is vegetable eater," Pyotr said.

"Lots of people are vegetarians, but that doesn't make them burglars," Kate said. She braced her feet against the floor; they were approaching an amber light. "Besides, she's not really a vegetarian; she just says she is."

Pyotr sped up even faster and sailed through the light. "She *is* a vegetarian," he said. "She made you take the meat from the mush-dish."

"Yes, but then she keeps stealing my beef jerky."

"She is stealing your beef jerky?"

"I have to change my hiding place every couple of days because she's always swiping it. She's no more vegetarian than I am! It's just one of those phases, one of those teenage fads. You have to tell the police she didn't do it, Pyotr. Tell them you made a mistake."

"Anyway," Pyotr said gloomily, "what is the difference who did it? Mice are vanished. All that care we took for them; now they are scampering the streets of Baltimore."

"You really think animal lovers would turn a bunch of cage-reared mice loose in city traffic? They do have *some* common sense. Those mice are stashed away someplace safe and protected, with all their antibodies or whatever perfectly intact."

"Please do not contradict me," Pyotr said.

Kate rolled her eyes at the ceiling, and neither one of them spoke again.

Dr. Battista's plan had been for Kate to start wearing her mother's wedding ring after the ceremony, and she had brought it with her to the church. But it had not been mentioned during the vows—a sign, perhaps, that Uncle Theron was more flustered by the general tumult than he had let on—and so now she bent and drew her billfold from her tote and took the ring out of the coin compartment. The wedding ring was yellow gold and her engagement ring was white gold, but her father had told her that was perfectly acceptable. She slipped it onto her finger and returned her billfold to her tote.

They zipped down North Charles, somehow managing to hit every intersection just as the traffic light was turning red. Pyotr never once stopped. They whizzed past cherry trees and Bradford pear trees in full bloom, each with a puddle of pink or white petals on the ground underneath. When they reached the construction mess around the Johns Hopkins campus, Pyotr took a snappy turn off Charles without bothering to signal, nearly mowing down a crowd of young people carrying picnic baskets. It was almost one o'clock now, and the whole world seemed to be heading out for lunch—everyone laughing, calling to friends, strolling aimlessly with no sense of urgency. Pyotr cursed under his breath and cranked his window shut.

In front of Mrs. Murphy's house, Pyotr scraped his tires alongside the curb and cut the engine. He opened his door and got out and nearly shut it on Kate's ankles, because she was in the act of sliding past the stick shift and across the driver's seat. "Watch it!" she told him. At least he had the grace then to stand back and wait for her to emerge, but he still didn't speak, and he closed the door with unnecessary firmness once she was out.

They smushed a layer of pale pink blossoms carpeting the sidewalk. They climbed the three brick steps and came to a stop on the stoop. Pyotr slapped his front pockets. Then he slapped his rear pockets. Then he said, "Hell damn," and put his finger on the doorbell and held it there.

It seemed at first that no one would answer. Finally, though, a creaking sound came from inside, and then Mrs. Liu flung the door open and demanded, "Why you ring?"

She was wearing what appeared to be the same clothes she had worn when Kate first met her, but she was no longer all smiles. Without giving Kate so much as a glance, she scowled fiercely at Pyotr and said, "Mrs. Murphy having her nap."

"I don't want Mrs. Murphy; I want to get into house!" Pyotr shouted.

"You have key to get into house!"

"I locked key in car!"

"Again? You do this again?"

"Do not *quack* at me! You are very rude!" And Pyotr shoved his way past her and strode directly to the staircase.

"Sorry," Kate told Mrs. Liu. "We didn't mean to disturb you. Monday I'm getting an extra key made, so this shouldn't happen again."

"*He* is the one is very rude," Mrs. Liu said.

"He's had a really hard day."

"He has many hard days," Mrs. Liu said. But she stepped back, finally, and let Kate enter the house. Belatedly, she asked, "You got married?"

"Right."

"Congratulations."

"Thanks," Kate said.

She hoped Mrs. Liu wasn't feeling sorry for her. Before, she had acted so fond of Pyotr, but now it seemed they disliked each other.

Pyotr had reached the second flight of stairs before she caught up with him. She bypassed him and started toward the room that was going to be hers, where she planned to deposit her tote. Behind her, Pyotr said, "Where my extra keys are?"

She paused and turned. He had stopped on the landing, and he was gazing all around him. Since the landing was entirely bare, without a stick of furniture or a picture or so much as a hook on the wall, it seemed an unlikely place to look for his keys, but there he stood, wearing a baffled expression.

She censored the first response that came to her, which was "How should *I* know where your extra keys are?" She set her tote on the floor and asked, "Where do you keep them?"

"In kitchen drawer," he said.

"Let's look in the kitchen drawer, then, why don't we," she said. She spoke more slowly and evenly than usual, so that she wouldn't come across as exasperated.

She led the way to the kitchen and began opening the cranky white metal drawers beneath the counter: one drawer containing dime-store knives and forks and spoons, one containing an assortment of cooking utensils, one containing dishcloths. She returned to the utensil drawer. That seemed to have the most possibilities, even if it wasn't where she herself would have kept keys. She rattled through several spatulas, a whisk, a hand-cranked eggbeater . . . Pyotr stood watching with his arms hanging limp, offering no help.

"Here you go," she said finally, and she held up an aluminum shower-curtain ring bearing a house key and a Volkswagen key.

Pyotr said, "Ah!" and lunged for them, but she took a step back and hid the keys behind her.

"First you have to call the police," she said, "and tell them you made a mistake about Bunny. *Then* you get the keys."

"What?" he said. "No. Hand me keys, Katherine. I am husband and I say hand me keys."

"I am wife and I say no," she said.

She supposed he could have wrested them from her. She fancied she saw the thought cross his face. But in the end he said, "I will only tell police Bunny is maybe not vegetarian. Okay?"

"Tell them she didn't take the mice."

"I will tell them you *think* she didn't take the mice."

Kate decided that was the best she could hope for. "Do it, then," she said.

He took his cell phone from the right front pocket of his shorts. Then he took his billfold from his back pocket. He pulled out a business card. "Detective assigned to my case, personally," he said with some pride. He held the card up for her to read. "How you pronounce this name?"

She peered at it. "McEnroe," she said.

"McEnroe." He clicked his phone on, studied the screen a moment, and then began the laborious process of placing a call.

Even from where she stood, she could hear the single ring, followed immediately by a male voice making a canned announcement. "He must have turned his phone off," she told Pyotr. "Leave a message."

Pyotr lowered his phone and gaped at her. "He turned it *off*?" he asked.

"That's why his voice mail picked up so fast. Leave a message."

"But he said I call him night or day. He said this was his personal number."

"Oh, for God's sake," she said. She snatched the phone away from him and pressed it to her ear. "Detective McEnroe, this is Kate Battista," she said. "I'm calling for Pyotr Shcherbakov; the laboratory break-in case. He told you that my sister, Bunny, could be a possible suspect, but that's because he was thinking Bunny's a vegetarian, and she's not. She eats meat. Also she was home all last evening and I'm sure I would have known if she had gone out during the night, so you can take her off your list. Thanks. Bye."

She ended the call and returned the phone to Pyotr. It was anyone's guess whether she had spoken in time to be recorded.

Pyotr put the phone in his pocket. He said, "Detective told me, 'Here's my card.' He told me, 'You should call me any time, if you have any further thoughts.' And now he does not answer. Is final straw; is last straw. This is worst day of my life."

Kate knew it was unreasonable of her, but she couldn't help feeling insulted.

She gave up the keys in silence.

"Thank you," he said absently. Then he said, "Well, thank you"—the unaccustomed "well" slightly softening his tone. He passed a hand over his face. He looked drawn and weary, and suddenly older than his age.

"I have not told you this," he said, "but the three years I have been here have been difficult years. Lonesome years. Perplexing. Everyone acts that to be in America is a gift, but is not one hundred percent a gift. Americans say things that are misleading. They seem so friendly; they use first names from beginning. They seem so casual and informal. Then they turn off their phones. I do not understand them!"

He and Kate were facing each other, no more than a foot apart. She was close enough to see the microscopic blond glints of his whiskers, and the tiny brown specks mixed in with the blue of his eyes.

"It is the language, maybe?" he asked. "I know the vocabulary, but still I am not capable to work the language the way I want to. There is no special word for 'you' when it is you that I am speaking to. In English there is only one 'you,' and I have to say the same 'you' to you that I would say to a stranger; I cannot express my closeness. I am homesick in this country, but I am thinking I would be homesick in my own country now, also. I have no longer any home to go back to—no relatives, no position, and my friends have lived three years without me. There is no *place* for me. So I have to pretend I am fine here. I have to pretend everything is . . . how you say? Hunky-dory."

Kate was reminded of her father's confession weeks earlier, when he was telling her what a long haul it had been. Men were just subject to this belief that they should keep their miseries buried deep inside, it seemed, as if admitting to them would be shameful. She reached out and touched Pyotr's arm, but he gave no sign he had noticed. "I bet you didn't even have breakfast," she told him. It was all she could think of to say. "That's what it is! You're starving. I'm going to fix you something."

"I don't want it," he said.

In the church she had been thinking that maybe the reason he went ahead with the wedding regardless was that underneath, he . . . well, liked her, a little. But now he wasn't even looking at her; he didn't seem to care that she was standing there so close to him with her hand on his arm. "I just want mice back," he said.

Kate dropped her hand.

"I would *like* that the thief would be Bunny," he said. "Then she could tell us where are they."

Kate said, "Believe me, Pyotr, it wasn't Bunny. Bunny's nothing but a copycat! She just has this little semi-crush or whatever it is on Edward Mintz and so when Edward said he was vegan . . ."

She paused. Pyotr was still not looking at her or even hearing her, probably. "Oh," she said. "It was Edward."

Then he did flick his eyes in her direction.

"Edward knows where the lab is," she said. "He went to the lab with Bunny, that time she brought Father his lunch. He must have been standing right beside her when she punched in the lock combination."

Pyotr had been holding the keys in his left hand, and now he gave them a sudden toss upward, caught them again, and walked out of the kitchen.

Kate said, "Pyotr?"

By the time she reached the landing, he was halfway down the first flight of stairs. "Where are you going?" she called over the railing. "Just wait till you've finished lunch and then call the detective, why don't you. What do you think you're doing? Can I come with you?"

But all she heard was the slapping sound of his flip-flops descending the stairs.

She should *make* him take her with him. She should run after him and fling herself into the car. It was hurt feelings, probably, that stopped her. Ever since the wedding he had been downright abusive, as if now that they were married he thought he could treat her however he liked. He hadn't even noticed how helpful she had been about his stupid keys, or how she had offered so nicely to fix him something to eat.

She turned from the stairs and continued down the hall to the living room. She went over to one of the windows and peered at the street below. The VW was already pulling away from the curb.

IN MOVIES, WOMEN were always flinging together elegant, impromptu meals from odds and ends in the fridge, but Kate didn't see how she could do that with what was in Pyotr's fridge. All it held was a jar of mayonnaise, a few cans of beer, a carton of eggs, and some very pale celery. Also a screwed-up bag from McDonald's, which she didn't bother investigating. The fruit bowl on the counter displayed a single speckled banana. "Miracle food," she could hear Pyotr saying, which seemed at odds with his fondness for McDonald's and KFC. When she looked through the cupboards above the counter she found rows and rows of empty containers—bottles and jars and jugs meticulously washed and saved. You would think he planned to take up canning.

Her only option was scrambled eggs, she figured, but then she realized he didn't even have butter. Could you make scrambled eggs with no butter? She wasn't going to risk it. Maybe deviled, then. At least he had mayonnaise. She put four eggs in the dented saucepan she found in the drawer beneath the stove, and she covered them with water and set them to boil.

She hoped he wasn't doing anything foolish. He should have just called the police. But maybe that was where he was going, down to the station in person, or maybe to the lab to reconnoiter with her father.

She went back to the living room and looked out the window again, for no earthly reason.

The living room seemed less empty now that Pyotr had moved his desk in from the study. It was heaped with various belongings that must also have been in the study—junk mail and stacks of books and coiled extension cords, in addition to the computer equipment. She picked up a wall calendar, curious to know if he'd made a note of their wedding, but the page was still turned to February and all the days were blank. She put it back on the desk.

She returned to the landing for her tote and carried it to her room. The leopard-print slipcover had vanished; the daybed had been stripped to its rust-stained navy-and-white-striped mattress, and there was no sign of sheets or blankets. A naked pillow slumped on the floor next to it. Couldn't he at least have put fresh linens on—tried to make it more welcoming? Her garment bag hung in the closet and her carton of shower gifts sat on the bureau, but she couldn't imagine ever feeling she belonged here.

The air in this room had an atticky smell, and she walked over to the window and struggled to open it, but it wouldn't budge. Finally she gave up and went back out to the kitchen. She looked to see if the eggs were done, but how was she supposed to tell? At home she had relied on a plastic color-changing gadget dating back to Mrs. Larkin. So she let the eggs cook a few minutes longer while she spooned mayonnaise into a plastic mixing bowl and sprinkled in salt and pepper from the two shakers on the table. Then she resumed her inventory, looking into all the under-counter cabinets, but they were nearly empty. After lunch, she would have to unpack the kitchen items from her box of shower gifts. The thought lifted her spirits somewhat. A project! She knew just where she would store her green mugs.

She turned off the burner beneath the eggs and carried the pan to the sink and ran cold water over them until they were cool enough to handle. When she started peeling the first one she could tell by the feel of the white that it was cooked enough, but as luck would have it, the shell came off in tiny, sharp, stubborn chips, bringing chunks of white along with them. The egg ended up about half its original size, pockmarked and ugly, and the tips of her fingers were bleeding. She said, "Damn," and rinsed the egg under the faucet and held it up, considering.

All right, egg salad, then.

This turned out to be a wise decision, because the other three eggs looked equally deformed after she had peeled them. She chopped them with a very dull knife and then she chopped some celery, using the counter as her work surface because she couldn't find a cutting board. Most of the celery had to be stripped off and thrown into the bucket under the sink. Even the innermost stalks were slightly flabby.

She thought of the salad bowl she'd been given at her shower, and she went back to her room to get it. Packed inside the bowl was her dream catcher. She took it out and held it up and pivoted slowly in the center of the room, debating where to hang it. Ideally, she supposed, it should be suspended from the ceiling directly over her bed, but that seemed like a lot of work and she wasn't sure that Pyotr owned a hammer and nails. She looked toward the window. It had only a yellowed paper shade, but there must have been curtains at some point because an adjustable metal rod was stretched between brackets above it. She put the dream catcher down and dragged the ottoman over from in front of the armchair in the corner. Then she took off her shoes and stood on the ottoman and tied the dream catcher to the curtain rod.

She wondered if Pyotr had ever seen one of these. He would probably find it peculiar. Well, it *was* peculiar. He would fold his arms and tilt his head and study it for a long, silent moment. Things always seemed to interest him so. He always seemed to be watching her with such close attention—at least until today. She wasn't accustomed to attention, but she couldn't say she found it unpleasant.

She hopped off the ottoman and dragged it back to the armchair and put her shoes on again.

Could the police have had him come with them to Edward's house to make the arrest, possibly?

It was almost 2:30. The so-called wedding banquet was scheduled for 5:00. This meant there was plenty of time yet, but on the other hand, Aunt Thelma's house was way out in horse country and Pyotr would need to wash up and change clothes before he went. And Kate was all too familiar with how people in labs could forget to look at the clock.

Maybe he had to fill something out, a warrant or an affidavit or whatever they called it.

She unpacked the rest of her shower gifts and found places for them in the kitchen. She emptied her suitcases into her bureau drawers, helter-skelter at first, but then, feeling time hanging heavy, she rearranged everything in orderly stacks. She unpacked the items from her tote— her brush and comb, which she set on her bureau; her toothbrush, which she took to the bathroom. It seemed too intimate, somehow, to fit her toothbrush into the holder alongside Pyotr's, so she went to the kitchen for a jelly glass and she stood her toothbrush in that and set it on the bathroom windowsill. There was no medicine cabinet, but a narrow wooden shelf above the sink held shaving supplies, a comb, and a tube of toothpaste. Would they be sharing this toothpaste? Should she have brought her own? How, exactly, were they going to divide the household expenses?

There were so many logistics they hadn't thought to discuss.

Next to the shower stall, a used-looking towel and washcloth hung on a chrome rod, and on another rod next to the toilet were another towel and washcloth, brand new. Those must be meant for her. The sight partly assuaged the injury of the bare mattress in her bedroom.

It was after 3:00 now. She took her phone from her

tote and checked it, just in case she'd somehow missed his call, but there were no messages. She put the phone back. She would just go ahead and eat on her own. All at once she was hungry.

In the kitchen she scooped a bit of egg salad onto a chipped white plate. She got herself a fork and a paper towel, since she couldn't find any napkins, and she settled herself at the table. But when she looked down at her lunch she caught sight of a fleck of bright red on a piece of yolk: her own blood. She spotted another fleck, and another. In fact, her egg salad as a whole looked effortful and not quite clean—overhandled. She stood up and scraped her serving into the garbage bucket, and she added the rest of the egg salad from the bowl and then concealed the whole mess beneath the paper towel. The kitchen had no dishwasher, so she rinsed her dishes under the tap and dried them with another paper towel and put them away. Destroying the evidence.

It occurred to her that life in the coed dorm had been a lot more fun than this. Also (looking down at her left hand) that white gold and yellow gold really didn't go together. What had she been thinking, listening to her father on matters of fashion? In fact, people shouldn't wear rings at all if their nails were short and ragged and rimmed with garden soil.

From the fridge she took a beer, and she opened it and tossed back a good portion of it before she went out to the landing again, still carrying the can. She wandered toward Pyotr's room. His door was shut, but what the hell; she turned the knob and walked in.

The room was sparsely furnished, like the rest of the apartment, and very neat. The only thing out of place was the ironing board that had been set up at the room's center, with an iron standing on top of it and a crisp white dress shirt draped over its narrower end. This had the same effect on her as the new towel and washcloth. She felt more hopeful.

The double bed beneath the window was covered with a red satin quilt stitched with fraying gold thread, like something in a cheap motel, and a reading lamp was clamped precariously to the headboard. On the night-stand was a bottle of aspirin and a gilt-framed photo of Kate. Of Kate? She picked it up. Oh, of Kate and Pyotr, except that since Kate's stool was higher than Pyotr's chair she filled more of the scene. The startled expression she wore wrinkled her forehead unbecomingly, and the T-shirt beneath her buckskin jacket was streaked with dirt. It was not a picture to be proud of. All that distin-guished it from the others her father had snapped—some at least marginally more flattering—was that it was the very first one, the one he'd taken on the day that she and Pyotr had met.

She thought about that a moment and then set the picture back down on the nightstand.

The bureau was topped with a dusty cutwork dresser scarf, probably Mrs. Liu's contribution, and a saucer that contained a few coins and a single safety pin. Nothing else. The walnut-framed mirror above it was so old that Kate seemed to be looking at herself through gauze—

her face suddenly pale and her cloud of black hair almost gray. She took another swig of beer and opened a drawer.

It was her superstitious belief that people who snooped in other people's private spaces were punished with hurtful discoveries, but Pyotr's drawers revealed just a paltry collection of clothing, carefully folded and stacked. There were two long-sleeved jerseys she had seen a dozen times, two short-sleeved polo shirts, a small pile of socks rolled in pairs (all ribbed white athletic socks except for one pair of navy dress socks), several pairs of white knit underpants like the ones the little boys in Room 4 wore, and several foreign-looking, tissue-thin undershirts with uncommonly close-set straps. No pajamas. No accessories, no doodads, no frivolities. The only thing she learned about him was the touching meagerness of his life. The meagerness and the . . . rectitude, was the word that came to her mind.

In his closet she found the suit he must have been planning to wear to the wedding—a shiny navy—along with two pairs of jeans, one still threaded with a belt. A vivid purple tie splashed with yellow lightning bolts was looped over the rod, and his brown Oxfords sat on the floor beside his sneakers.

Kate took another swig of beer and left the room.

Back in the kitchen, she polished off her beer and tossed the can into the paper bag that Pyotr appeared to be using for recycling. She got another beer from the fridge and returned to her own room.

She went directly to her closet and unzipped the

garment bag and lifted out the dress she planned to wear to Aunt Thelma's. It was the one piece of clothing she owned that seemed suitable for a party—red cotton with a scoop neck. She hung it from the hook on the closet door and stepped back to assess it. Should she give it a touch-up with Pyotr's iron? That seemed like a lot of work, though. She took a meditative sip of beer and gave up on the idea.

The walls here in her bedroom were as bare as the others. She had never realized how bleak a place looked without pictures. For a few minutes, she entertained herself by contemplating what she might hang. Some things from her room at home, maybe? But those were so outdated—faded posters featuring rock groups she no longer listened to, and team photos from her basketball days. She should find something new. Start fresh.

But this time, the thought of a project failed to perk her up. She was feeling very tired, all at once. It might have been the beer, or it might have been because she had slept poorly the night before, but she wished she could take a nap. If there had been sheets on the bed, she *would* have taken a nap. As it was, she sat down in the armchair in the corner, and she kicked her shoes off and stretched her legs out on the ottoman. Even through the closed window, she could hear birds singing. She focused on those. "Terwhilliker, whilliker, whilliker!" they seemed to be saying. Gradually, her eyelids grew heavy. She set her beer can down on the floor and let herself drift into sleep.

❧

FOOTSTEPS COMING UP the stairs, *slap-slap-slap.* "Khello?" Footsteps across the landing. "Where *are* you?" Pyotr called. A giant peony bush arrived in her doorway, with Pyotr somewhere behind it. "Oh. You are resting," he said.

She couldn't see his face because it was hidden by the bush, which stood in a green plastic nursery pot and already had some buds on it. White, they were going to be. She sat up straighter. She felt a little muzzy. It had been a mistake to drink beer in the daytime.

"What happened?" she asked him.

Instead of answering, he said, "Why you didn't rest on your bed?" Then he slapped the side of his head, nearly losing control of the peony bush. "The sheets," he said. "I bought new sheets, and new sheets have toxic chemicals perhaps, so I washed them. They are down in Mrs. Murphy's dryer."

This was absurdly heartening to hear. Kate reached for her shoes and slipped them on. "Did you tell the police?" she asked.

"Tell them what?" he said, infuriatingly. He was setting the peony bush on the floor, standing back to dust his hands off. "Oh," he said in a nonchalant tone. "Mice are back."

"They're . . . back?"

"After you say it is Eddie," he said, "I think, 'Yes. Makes sense. It is Eddie.' So I get in my car and I drive to his house and I pound on his door. 'Where my mice are?' I ask him. 'What mice?' he says. False surprised look, I can see right away. 'Just tell me you didn't loosen them in the streets,' I say. 'In the streets!' he says. 'Do you really think I'd be that cruel?' 'Tell me they are caged,' I say, 'wherever they are. Tell me you did not expose them to any common, *downtown* mice.' He gets pouty dark look on his face. 'They're safe in my room,' he says. His mother is shouting at me, but I do not pay heed. 'I'm calling the police!' she is shouting, but I run straight upstairs and find out which is his room. Mice are still in cages, stacked high."

"Whoa," Kate said.

"This is why I am gone so long. Making Eddie move mice back to lab. Your father was in lab. He hugged me! He had tears behind his glasses! Then Eddie became arrested, but your father is not, how they say? Pushing charges."

"Really!" Kate said. "Why not?"

Pyotr shrugged. "Long story," he said. "We decided after detective came. Detective answered his phone, this time! *Very* nice man. Lovely man. Plant is from Mrs. Liu."

"What?" Kate said. She was feeling as if she'd been spun in circles with a blindfold on.

"She asked that I carry it to you. Wedding present. Something for backyard."

"So she's okay now?" Kate asked.

"Okay?"

"She was in such a temper."

"Oh, yes, she is always talking mean when I lose my keys," he said blithely. He walked over to the window and lifted the sash with no apparent effort. "Ah!" he said. "Is lovely outside! Are we not late?"

"Excuse me?"

"Was reception not at five?"

Kate glanced at her watch: 5:20. "Oh, God," she said, and she leapt to her feet.

"Come! We drive fast. You can phone your aunt from car."

"But I'm not changed. *You're* not changed."

"We go as we are; it is family."

Kate spread her arms to reveal the wrinkles across the front of her dress from her nap, and the mayonnaise stain near her hem. "Just give me half a second, okay?" she said. "This dress is a disaster."

"Is a beautiful dress," he said.

She looked down at it and then dropped her arms. "Fine, it's a beautiful dress," she said. "Have it your way."

But he was already out on the landing now, heading toward the stairs, and she had to run to catch up with him.

CHAPTER TWELVE

AUNT THELMA ANSWERED THE DOOR IN A FLOOR-
length, flowered hostess gown. Kate could smell her per-
fume even from where they stood. "Hello, my dears!" she
cried. There was no way she could not have been taken
aback by what they were wearing, but she hid it well.
She stepped out onto the veranda to press her cheek to
Kate's and then to Pyotr's. "Welcome to your wedding
banquet!"

"Thank you, Aunt Sel," Pyotr said, and he flung
his arms around her in an enthusiastic hug that nearly
knocked her over.

"Sorry we're so late," Kate told her. "Sorry we didn't
have time to dress."

"Well, you're here; that's all that matters," her aunt
said—a much milder reaction than Kate would have predicted. She patted down the side of her hairdo that Pyotr
had disarranged. "Come on out back; everyone's having
drinks. Aren't we lucky the weather's so nice!"

She turned to lead them through the entrance hall,
which was two stories high. A giant crystal chandelier
hung at its center like an upside-down Christmas tree,
and Pyotr slowed to gaze up at it for a moment with a
dazzled expression. In the living room, sectional couches

lumbered through the vast space like a herd of rhinos, and both coffee tables were the size of double beds. "Kate's father has been telling us what an eventful day you've had, Pyoder," Aunt Thelma said.

"Was *very* eventful," Pyotr said.

"He's been quite talkative, for him. We've all learned the most amazing amount about mice."

She opened the French doors to the patio. It was a long while yet till sunset, but paper lanterns glowed in the trees and netted candles flickered palely on all the tables. When Kate and Pyotr stepped out onto the flagstones, the guests turned as a group, which made it seem as if there were considerably more of them than there really were. Kate felt the force of their attention like a wind that suddenly smacked her in the face. She stopped short, holding her tote low in front of her to hide the mayonnaise stain. "Here they are!" Aunt Thelma caroled, and she flung out one arm majestically. "Introducing . . . Mr. and Mrs. Cherbakov and Cherbakova! Or however they do it."

There was a general "Ah!" and a smattering of applause, most people just patting the insides of their wrists with their fingertips in order to accommodate their wineglasses. Kate's girlhood friend Alice had put on a little weight since Kate had last seen her, and her husband held a baby perched in the crook of his arm. Uncle Theron was wearing a defiantly unchurchy outfit of khakis and a Hawaiian shirt, but all the other men wore suits, and the women were in spring dresses that showed their winter-white arms and legs.

Dr. Battista was clapping the loudest. He had set his glass on a table to free his hands, and his face was shining with emotion. Bunny, at the far end of the patio, wasn't clapping at all. She clenched a Pepsi can in her fist and glared at Pyotr and Kate belligerently.

"All right, everybody, we're switching to champagne," Uncle Barclay called. He arrived in front of Pyotr and Kate with two foam-topped flutes. "Drink up; it's the good stuff," he told them.

"Thanks," Kate said, accepting hers, and Pyotr said, "Thank you, Uncle Bark."

"Looks like *you* just got out of bed, Pyoder," Uncle Barclay said with a sly chuckle.

"This is the latest fashion," Kate told him. She'd be damned if she would offer any more apologies. "He bought it at Comme des Garçons."

"Beg your pardon?"

She took a hefty sip of champagne.

"Could you and Pyoder stand closer together?" her father asked her. He was holding his cell phone in both hands. "I can't believe I didn't get any pictures of the wedding. I know I had a lot on my mind, but . . . Maybe your uncle could restage the ceremony for us."

"No," Kate told him flatly.

"No? Oh, well," he said, squinting down at his phone. "Whatever you say, darling. This is such a joyous day! And you are the one we have to thank, pointing us toward the Mintz boy. I never would have suspected him."

He was snapping more photographs as he spoke; he'd begun to look less incompetent at it. But there was no hope that the results would be any better, because Kate had her nose buried in her glass and Pyotr was turning away to snag a canapé from the tray Aunt Thelma was offering. "Maybe I take two," he was saying. "I have not had breakfast or lunch."

"Oh, you poor thing! Take three," Aunt Thelma said. "Louis? Caviar?"

"No, never mind that. Barclay, could you snap a picture of me with the bride and groom?"

"Be glad to," Uncle Barclay said, at the same time that Aunt Thelma told him, "First you have to see to everybody's champagne. Kate's already drinking hers, and we haven't even had the toast yet."

Kate lowered her glass guiltily, although really it was Uncle Barclay's fault. He was the one who had told her to drink up.

Her father said, "The thing that gets me is, I still don't understand why this happened. This thing with the animal people, I mean. My mice lead enviable lives! More healthful than many humans' lives, in fact. I've always had a very good relationship with my mice."

"Well, better with them than with no one, I suppose," Aunt Thelma said, and she sailed off with her tray.

Aunt Thelma's son, Richard, was making his way toward them with his wife, a pale, icy blonde with poreless skin and pearly pink lips. Kate tugged at her father's sleeve and whispered, "Quick: what's Richard's wife's name?"

"You're asking *me*?"

"It starts with an *L*. Leila? Leah?"

"Cuz!" Richard said jovially. He wasn't usually so friendly. "Congratulations! Congratulations, Pyoder," he said, slapping him jarringly on the back. "I'm Kate's cousin, Richard. This is my wife, Jeannette."

Dr. Battista raised his eyebrows at Kate. Pyotr said, "Rich, I am glad to meet you. Jen, I am glad to meet you."

Kate waited for Richard to draw one of his nose-breaths in protest, but he let it pass. "Can't believe we're finally marrying this gal off," he said. "Whole family's beside themselves with relief."

Since this confirmed Kate's worst suspicions, she felt stabbed to the heart. And Jeannette said, "Oh, *Richard*," which somehow made it worse.

Pyotr said, "I too am relieved. I did not know if Kate would like me."

"Well, sure she would! You're her own kind, right?"

"I am her kind?"

Richard suddenly looked less sure of himself, but he said, "I mean you're in that same milieu or whatever. That science milieu she was raised in. Right, Uncle Louis?" he asked. "No *normal* person could understand you people."

"What exactly do you find difficult to understand?" Dr. Battista asked him.

"Oh, you know, all that science jargon; I can't off-hand—"

"I am researching autoimmune disorders," Dr. Battista said. "It's true that 'autoimmune' has four syllables, but perhaps if I broke the word down for you . . ."

Kate felt somebody slip an arm around her waist, and she started. She turned to find Alice standing next to her, smiling and saying, "Congratulations, stranger."

"Thanks," Kate said.

"I wouldn't have missed this for the world. How've you *been*?"

"I'm okay."

"Have you seen my little lambie pie over there?"

"Yes, I noticed. Is it a boy or a girl?"

Alice frowned. "She's a girl, of course," she said. Then she brightened and said, "Hurry up and have one of your own now, so they can be playmates."

"Oh, gosh," Kate said. She looked around for the canapés, but they were clear across the patio.

"So tell me about your guy! Where'd you meet him? How long have you known him? He's very sexy."

"He works in my father's lab," Kate said. "We've known each other three years." This was beginning to feel like the truth, she realized. She could almost summon up some concrete memories from their long acquaintance.

"Are those two over there his parents?"

"What? Oh, no, that's the Gordons," Kate said. "Our neighbors from two doors down. Pyotr doesn't have any parents. He doesn't have any family at all."

"Lucky," Alice said. "I mean, sad for *him*, of course, but lucky for you: no in-laws to deal with. You should meet Jerry's mother sometime." She flashed a huge toothy smile toward her husband and trilled her fingers at him.

"She thinks he should have married his girlfriend the neurosurgeon," she said through her smile.

Uncle Barclay stepped out to the center of the patio and called, "Everyone have champagne now?"

There was a general murmur.

"Like to propose a toast, then," he said. "Pyoder and Katherine! May you two be as happy as your aunt and I have been."

Little cheers rose up here and there, and everyone took a sip. Kate had no idea what to do in response. In fact, she had never been toasted before. So she just tipped her glass to them all and nodded, and then she slid her eyes toward Pyotr to see what *he* was doing. He was grinning from ear to ear. He was holding his glass sky-high, and then he lowered it and threw back his head and drained his champagne in one gulp.

For her seating arrangements at dinner, Aunt Thelma proceeded as if they were in a formal banquet hall—the bride and groom placed next to each other at the center of one long side of the table, with members of the family aligned to their right and left in descending order of relatedness. It was sort of like *The Last Supper*.

"Your father will be on your right," Aunt Thelma told Kate as she ushered her into the dining room, although she really didn't need to explain, because elegantly calligraphed name cards stood at the head of each plate. "Bunny's on Pyoder's left. Then I'll sit on your father's other side and Barclay will sit on Bunny's other side. Theron's at this end of the table and Richard's at that end, and everyone else is boy-girl-boy-girl on the side across from you."

But there were problems. First, Bunny refused to sit next to Pyotr. She walked into the dining room and took one look at the place cards and said, "I am not sitting anywhere near that person. Trade seats with me, Uncle Barclay."

Uncle Barclay looked surprised, but he was good-natured about it. "Sure thing," he said, drawing back his chair for her, and then he settled himself in the chair next to Pyotr's. "Looks like sister-in-law troubles ahead for *you*, my friend," he murmured to Pyotr.

"Yes, she is very enraged at me," Pyotr said equably.

Kate leaned closer to her father, who was unfolding his napkin. "What is she enraged about?" she whispered. "I thought you didn't press charges."

"It's complicated," her father said.

"Complicated how?"

Her father merely shrugged and smoothed his napkin across his lap.

Then Alice didn't like *her* seat assignment, although she was less emphatic about it. She was supposed to sit on the long side opposite Kate and Pyotr, but she sidled up to Aunt Thelma and said, "I hate to ask this, but could I be moved to an end place, please?"

Aunt Thelma said, "An end place?"

"I'm going to have to nurse my baby at some point, and I'll need some elbow room."

"Certainly," Aunt Thelma said. "Richard, dear?" she called. "Could you trade seats with Alice?"

Richard wasn't as accommodating as Uncle Barclay had been. "Why?" he asked.

"She needs room to nurse her baby, dear."

"Nurse her *baby*?"

Aunt Thelma slipped gracefully into the seat on the other side of Kate's father. Richard, after a significant pause, stood up and moved one seat over, next to Mr. Gordon, and Alice settled at the end of the table and held out her hands for her baby.

Kate was beginning to develop a certain grudging respect for Aunt Thelma. It was something like her second, grown-up viewing of *Gone with the Wind*, when Melanie had all at once struck her as the true heroine. In fact, she almost regretted not inviting her aunt to the wedding. Although probably that was just as well, in view of what a disaster it had been.

Pyotr and Kate were sitting close enough so that he could nudge her with his elbow anytime he wanted her to share his appreciation of something. And he found plenty to appreciate. He liked the vichyssoise that was served at the start—anything that featured potatoes or cabbage made him happy, Kate had learned—and the rack of lamb that came next. He liked the Bach partita that was playing over Uncle Barclay's sound system, as well as the sound system itself, with its four discreet speakers positioned in the four corners of the crown molding. He especially liked it when Alice's baby spit up just as Alice raised her high in the air to show her off. That made him actually laugh out loud, although Kate gave *him* a nudge then, to shut him up. And when Uncle Theron told Mrs. Gordon that his choir director had been "phoning it in" lately, Pyotr was ecstatic. "'Phoning it in!'" he repeated to Kate, jostling her as she was slicing her lamb. The knob of his elbow against her bare arm felt warm and calloused.

On her other side, her father suddenly bent over. He seemed to be trying to crawl underneath the table. "What are you *doing*?" Kate asked him, and he said, "I'm looking for that bag of yours."

"What do you want with it?"

"I just need to slip these papers in," he said. Briefly, he displayed them—several sheets folded in thirds like a business letter. Then he ducked his head under the table again. "Papers for the immigration people," he said in a muffled voice.

"Oh, for God's sake," Kate snapped, and she stabbed a bite of meat more forcefully than she needed to.

"Louis? Have you lost something?" Aunt Thelma called.

"No, no," he said. He sat up. His face was flushed from his effort, and his glasses had slipped down the bridge of his nose. "Just putting a little something in Kate's bag," he said.

"Oh, yes," Aunt Thelma said approvingly. She probably thought he meant money; that was how little she knew him. "I must say, Louis: you've done comparatively well with these girls," she told him. "All things considered." And she inclined her wineglass toward him. "I'll have to hand you that much. I know I told you at the time that you should give them to *me* to raise, but I see you might have been right to insist on keeping them with you."

Kate stopped chewing.

"Yes, well," Dr. Battista said. He turned to Kate and said, in a lower tone, "I suppose all the bureaucratese will seem a bit daunting at first, but I've included a business card with Morton Stanfield's phone number on it. He's an immigration lawyer and he's going to help you through this."

"Okay," Kate said. Then she patted his hand and said, "Okay, Father."

Alice was asking Bunny to cut her meat up for her, since she was nursing her baby now under cover of her draped cardigan. Jeannette was trying to catch Richard's eye; he had just poured himself what must have been at least his third glass of wine. She kept leaning forward and holding up an index finger like someone wishing to propose an amendment, but he had his gaze trained studiously elsewhere. Mrs. Gordon was telling Pyotr how sorry she was to hear that the Mintz boy had kidnapped his mice. She was seated on the other side of the table from Pyotr and several places down, so she needed to raise her voice. "Jim and Sonia Mintz should really step up to the plate," she called, and Kate flinched, because Bunny had to have overheard her.

"'Step up to the plate,'" Pyotr repeated in a musing tone.

"Batter's plate," Uncle Barclay advised him. "As in baseball."

"Ah! Nice. Very useful. I was thinking dinner plate."

"No, no."

"Even when Edward was little," Mrs. Gordon was saying, "Jim and Sonia were so *laissez-faire*. He was a peculiar child from the outset, but did they notice?"

"It sounds they were phoning it in," Pyotr told her.

He looked so happy as he said this, so obviously pleased with himself, that Uncle Barclay started laughing. "You really like our American expressions, Pyoder, don't you," he said, and Pyotr laughed too and said, "I *love* them!" His whole face was alight.

"Good man," Uncle Barclay said affectionately. "Here's to my man Pyoder!" he announced, holding up his wineglass. "Let's welcome him into the family."

There was a general stir around the table, with people chiming in and reaching for their own glasses, but before they could go any further, Bunny's chair screeched across the parquet and she jumped to her feet. "Well, *I* don't welcome him," she said. "There's no way on earth I'm going to welcome a guy who assaulted an innocent man."

Kate said, "Innocent!" and then, in a kind of double-take, "Assaulted?"

"He told me what you did!" Bunny said, turning on Pyotr. "You couldn't just ask him nicely to give you back your mice; oh, no. You had to go and sock him."

All the guests were staring at her.

"You socked him?" Kate asked Pyotr.

"He was a small bit reluctant to let me into his house," Pyotr said.

Bunny said, "You almost broke his jaw! Maybe you

did break his jaw. His mother's thinking now she should take him to the emergency room."

"Good," Pyotr said, buttering a slice of bread. "Maybe they wire his mouth shut."

Bunny asked the others, "Did you hear that?" and Dr. Battista said, "Now, Bun-Buns. Now, dear one. Control yourself, dear." And at the same time Kate was asking, "*What* happened? Wait."

"He practically batters the Mintzes' door down," Bunny told her, "yells at Edward right in his face and grabs him by his shirtfront; gives poor Mrs. Mintz a heart attack, just about, and then when Edward tries to block his path as of *course* he'd try—it's his private house— Pyoder knocks him flat on his back and goes storming up the stairs barging in and out of the Mintzes' personal bedrooms till finally he finds Edward's room and he shouts, 'Come up here! Come up this instant!' and he forces Edward to help him carry all the cages down the stairs and out to the Mintzes' minivan and when Mrs. Mintz says, 'What is this? Stop this!' he tells her, 'Get out of the way!' in this loud obnoxious voice. When *she* didn't know! She thought Edward was just keeping the mice for a friend! And he *was* keeping them for a friend, this man he'd met on the Internet from an organization in Pennsylvania, who was going to come down next week and take the mice to this no-kill shelter where they could be adopted, he said—"

Dr. Battista groaned, no doubt picturing his precious mice in the hands of a bunch of germ-ridden Pennsylvanians.

"—and then after they drive to the lab, and Edward is very helpful about unloading them from the minivan and putting them back in the mouse room, which is no easy task, believe me, what thanks does he get? Pyoder calls the police. He calls the police on him, after Edward has totally undone the damage. Right this very minute Edward would be rotting in jail, I bet, if Mrs. Mintz hadn't as it turned out called the police on *Pyoder*."

Kate said, "What?"

"I told you it was complicated," her father said.

The other diners looked spellbound. Even Alice's baby was staring at Bunny open-mouthed.

"There is poor Edward," Bunny said, "severely injured; one whole side of his face is swelled up like a pumpkin, so of *course* his mother called the police. Which means Father here"—and Bunny turned to Dr. Battista; it was the first time in years that Kate had heard her call him "Father"—"*Father* had to drop the charges, thank heaven, or else the Mintzes said they would press charges on Pyoder. It was a plea bargain."

Uncle Barclay said, "Well, I don't think that's exactly what they call a—"

"*That's* why you didn't press charges?" Kate asked her father.

"It seemed expedient," he said.

"But Pyotr was provoked!" Kate said. "It wasn't *his* fault he had to hit Edward."

"Is true," Pyotr said, nodding.

Aunt Thelma said, "In any event—"

"Naturally you would say that," Bunny told Kate.

"Naturally you would think Pyoder can do no wrong. It's like you've turned into some kind of zombie. 'Yes, Pyoder; no, Pyoder,' following him around all moony. 'Whatever you say, Pyoder; I'll do anything you like, Pyoder; certainly I'll marry you, Pyoder, even if all you're after is any old U.S. citizen,' you tell him. Then you show up super-late for your own wedding reception and the two of you are not even dressed, looking all mussed and rumpled like you've spent the afternoon making out. It's disgusting, is what it is. You'll never see *me* backing down like that when *I* have a husband."

Kate stood up and set her napkin aside. "Fine," she said. She was conscious of Pyotr's eyes on her—of everybody's eyes—and of Uncle Barclay's highly entertained expression and Aunt Thelma's tensed posture as she watched for the first possible chance to break in and put an end to this. But Kate focused solely on Bunny. "Treat your husband any way you like," she said, "but I pity him, whoever he is. It's *hard* being a man. Have you ever thought about that? Anything that's bothering them, men think they have to hide it. They think they should seem in charge, in control; they don't dare show their true feelings. No matter if they're hurting or desperate or stricken with grief, if they're heartsick or they're homesick or some huge dark guilt is hanging over them or they're about to fail big-time at something—'Oh, I'm okay,' they say. 'Everything's just fine.' They're a whole lot less free than women are, when you think about it. Women have been studying people's feelings since they were toddlers; they've been perfecting their radar—their intuition or their empathy or their interpersonal what-chamacallit. They know how things work underneath, while men have been stuck with the sports competitions and the wars and the fame and success. It's like men and women are in two different countries! I'm not 'backing down,' as you call it; I'm letting him into my country. I'm giving him space in a place where we can both be ourselves. Lord have mercy, Bunny, cut us some *slack*!"

Bunny sank onto her chair, looking dazed. She might not have been persuaded, but she was giving up the fight, for now.

Pyotr rose to his feet and placed an arm around Kate's shoulders. He smiled into her eyes and said, "Kiss me, Katya."

And she did.

EPILOGUE

LOUIE SHCHERBAKOV HAD A DEAL WITH HIS PARents where if they were leaving him with a sitter, he got to fix his own supper. Already he could cook a whole lot better than his mom, and almost as well as his dad. This fall when he entered first grade they were going to start letting him use the stove as long as a grown-up was around, but meanwhile he was allowed the microwave and the toaster oven, and silverware knives but not sharp knives. He was pretty good at cutting up beef jerky with the kitchen shears.

Tonight his parents were going to Washington because his mother was getting a prize. She had won a Plant Ecology Award from the Botanical Federation. All week, Louie had been telling people this. "Mom's getting a prize from the *Butt*-anical Federation," he would say, and then he would fall on the floor laughing. Most people just smiled politely, but if his dad was within hearing he would laugh as hard as Louie. When his dad laughed, his eyes would tip up at the outside corners. Louie's eyes did that too, and he had his dad's straight yellow hair. His mom's aunt Thelma said he looked so much like his dad that it was comical, but Louie didn't see what was comical about it. Was she talking about he didn't have big arm muscles like his dad's arm muscles? But he was getting there.

He put two slices of bread in the toaster oven, and then he hauled the stepstool over to the food cupboard and reached down a can of sardines. He wasn't all that crazy about sardines, but he liked opening the can with its little tin key. After he'd done that, he took a banana from the bowl on the counter because bananas were miracle food, and he peeled it and cut it into disks with a silverware knife. Then he went out on the landing and called, "Have we got any kidney beans?"

"What? No!" his mom called from his parents' bedroom.

"Too bad," he said, mostly to himself. He often ate kidney beans when he went to his grandpa's house, mashed up with a lot of other stuff. He liked the sourness of them.

"What on earth do you want with kidney beans?" his mom called, but then she added, in a lower voice, "I still don't see why I can't just wear pants."

"This is official occasion, though," his dad told her. "I myself am wearing suit."

"*You* try wearing a dress sometime. I look like a pet dog decked out by some demented child."

Louie went back to the kitchen and climbed up on the stepstool again and reached down the squeeze bottle of ketchup. Red would go good, he figured. Red, silver, and beige: ketchup, sardines, and bananas. "Where would be the green?" his dad always liked to ask, but his mom would say, "Oh, give it a rest. I've known kids who ate nothing but foods that were white until they left for college, and they were perfectly healthy."

Most times Louie's grandpa was his sitter, now that Aunt Bunny had married her personal trainer and moved to New Jersey. His grandpa owned a very old and faded book called *Curious Science Facts for Young Folks*, and when he came to sit he brought it along to read to Louie, which made Louie feel important and cared for even if he didn't exactly understand every single word. But tonight his grandpa would be going to Washington too, and so would Aunt Thelma and Uncle Barclay and Uncle Theron, so Louie was staying downstairs with Mrs. Liu. That was okay, though. Mrs. Liu let him drink Coca-Cola, and her friend Mrs. Murphy had these cool objects in her glass-fronted cabinet: a paperweight with gold stars swirling inside it instead of snowflakes, and a bright red berry with a top that opened to spill out a herd of microscopic white elephants, and a weather-house made of tan wood with a brown wooden roof. A tiny man or woman would come to one of the doors of the house— the woman if it was going to be sunny, the man if it was going to rain. Just about always it was the woman, though, holding her eentsy watering can, while the man stayed back in the shadows under his fingernail-size umbrella even when it was pouring. Louie's dad said it was a very inexact science.

Mrs. Liu wouldn't let his parents pay her for babysitting because she was Louie's auntie, she said. When he was little, Louie had thought she really *was* his aunt, on account of they had the same name, almost, but then his mom explained that Mrs. Liu was just an honorary aunt. And so was Mrs. Murphy, because this was her house they were living in even though Louie's grandpa wanted them to move in with him. But Louie's mom said she wasn't about to move. She said she'd lived here eleven years now and she was perfectly content, and what did they need more room for; it would only be more to vacuum, and his dad said she was absolutely right.

Louie took the toasts from the toaster oven and laid them on the counter. He covered one toast with banana disks and over those he laid sardines, all lined up, and then he drizzled ketchup on everything in a zigzag pattern. Finally he set the second slice of toast on top and pressed down hard, and he put the finished sandwich in a Tupperware sandwich box he got from a drawer. Smushing the sandwich had caused a little of the ketchup to squirt across the countertop, but not very much.

When his dad and his grandpa got *their* prize, last winter, it was in a whole other country and so Louie had had to go too. The ceremony was so boring that his mom let him play video games over and over on her cell phone. He wasn't sorry they were leaving him behind this time.

He licked his fingers off where he had smeared ketchup on them, and he tugged the dishtowel from the rack to wipe away as much as possible of the ketchup on his T-shirt. Meanwhile he could hear his parents' voices on the landing. "Don't let's stay a minute longer than we have to," his mom was saying. "You know how I hate chitchat," and then the two of them showed up at the kitchen door. His mom's long black hair was flaring out around her shoulders, and she wore her surprising red party dress with her two bare legs sticking out. His dad had his blue suit on and his pretty purple tie with the yellow lightning marks. "How do we look?" his mom asked, and Louie said, "You look like the weather-house people."

But then he saw that they didn't, really. It was true they were standing in a door, but they were both in the one door side by side and very close together, neither one in front or behind, and they were holding hands and smiling.

ABOUT THE AUTHOR

ANNE TYLER is the author of twenty best-selling novels. She was born in Minneapolis, Minnesota, in 1941 and grew up in Raleigh, North Carolina. She graduated at nineteen from Duke University and went on to do graduate work in Russian studies at Columbia University. *A Spool of Blue Thread*, Tyler's *New York Times* bestselling twentieth novel, was short-listed for the Man Booker Prize; her eleventh novel, *Breathing Lessons*, was awarded the Pulitzer Prize in 1988. She is a member of the American Academy of Arts and Letters. She lives in Baltimore, Maryland.

A READER'S GUIDE FOR *VINEGAR GIRL* BY ANNE TYLER

In order to provide reading groups with the most informed and thought-provoking questions possible, it is necessary to reveal certain aspects of the story in this novel. If you have not finished reading *Vinegar Girl*, we respectfully suggest that you do so before reviewing this guide.

QUESTIONS AND TOPICS FOR DISCUSSION

1. Compare and contrast Tyler's *Vinegar Girl* with Shakespeare's *The Taming of the Shrew*.

2. Do you think Tyler's Kate was less of a "shrew" than Shakespeare's Katherine?

3. Discuss Kate and Pyotr's first meeting. Did you think there was a connection or chemistry there from the beginning?

4. Did you like how Tyler transformed the misogynistic Petruchio to the quirky Pyotr? Do you think he was a good match for her sarcastic Kate?

5. Kate is unsatisfied with her life at home and at work, but has done nothing to change her situation. Do you think her father's strong suggestion to marry Pyotr was actually what she needed to change her life?

6. Discuss the character of Bunny and the role she plays in Kate's life.

7. Tyler is a master writer when it comes to depicting family relationships. Discuss the family dynamic in *Vinegar Girl*. Do you think all families struggle with the balance of acting selfishly and selflessly?

8. Were you surprised Kate was so upset when Pyotr did not show up to the church on time?

9. Discuss Kate's speech at the end of the novel. Do you agree with her?

10. What was your reaction to the story's epilogue? Is that how you imagined Kate's life to turn out?

THE HOGARTH SHAKESPEARE

For more than four hundred years, Shakespeare's works have been performed, read, and loved throughout the world. They have been reinterpreted for each new generation, whether as teen films, musicals, science-fiction flicks, Japanese warrior tales, or literary transformations.

The Hogarth Press was founded by Virginia and Leonard Woolf in 1917 with a mission to publish the best new writing of the age. In 2012, Hogarth was launched in London and New York to continue the tradition. The Hogarth Shakespeare project sees Shakespeare's works retold by acclaimed and bestselling novelists of today. The series launched in October 2015 and to date will be published in twenty countries.

THE TEMPEST
retold by
MARGARET ATWOOD

OTHELLO
retold by
TRACY CHEVALIER

HAMLET
retold by
GILLIAN FLYNN

THE MERCHANT OF VENICE
retold by
HOWARD JACOBSON

MACBETH
retold by
JO NESBØ

KING LEAR
retold by
EDWARD ST. AUBYN

THE TAMING OF THE SHREW
retold by
ANNE TYLER

THE WINTER'S TALE
retold by
JEANETTE WINTERSON

From *New York Times* Bestselling Author

ANNE TYLER

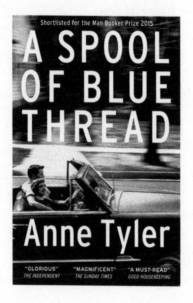

"An act of literary enchantment . . . Tyler remains among the best chroniclers of family life this country has ever produced."
—*Washington Post*

"A brilliant testament to why the novel still provides an enormously important role in our culture. . . . [A] noble artistic vision."
—*Toronto Star*

Available wherever books are sold